To Deborah,
Thank you for your love
and encouragement.
Love,
Irene Coté Single
Sept. 2014

Two
COUNTRIES,
Two
WOMEN

A Story Based on True Events of
Adventure, Faith, Tragedy, and Courage

IRENE COTE SINGLE

Inspiring Voices®

Inspiring Voices books may be ordered through booksellers or by contacting:

Inspiring Voices
1663 Liberty Drive
Bloomington, IN 47403
www.inspiringvoices.com
1 (866) 697-5313

ISBN: 978-1-4624-1024-8 (sc)
ISBN: 978-1-4624-1025-5 (e)

Library of Congress Control Number: 2014912892

Printed in the United States of America.

Inspiring Voices rev. date: 8/11/2014

This book is dedicated to my mom, Juliette A. Cote; her grandparents, parents, and siblings who inspired me; and to God for giving me life and the desire to write this story.

ACKNOWLEDGMENTS

A great big thank you to my husband, Bill, and daughter, Amber, for your support and encouragement in all the time it took to interview family and to finally pull everything together. I love you both dearly.

Thank you to my sister-in-law Jean who edited parts of my manuscript along the way and supported this venture in many ways.

Thank you to all my teachers, including the on-line and writing conference ones who taught me so much about writing. Eva Shaw and Dale Slongwhite, you are the best and I thank you for your confidence in me.

A special thank you goes to Sr. Helene Cote, PM, my spiritual director and friend, who believes in me and prayed with and for me for more than nine years.

Thank you to all my family and friends. You are too numerous to mention but I want to say I appreciate you all and love you with all my heart. Thanks for being part of my life and encouraging me to finish this project.

Thank you to Inspiring Voices for giving me the chance to publish my first book. You have been a great help in all aspects of publishing.

PREFACE

Dear Reader,

Several years ago I began my research about my mother's mother and grandmother and their families. I have been intrigued with the story of Mom's mother and maternal grandmother and wanted to write about them to pass on to the next generation. What I didn't realize is that it takes many interviews and many hours of research to accomplish this task. Also, in my effort to be as accurate as possible, it has sometimes become more of a burden than enjoyment.

Before I began these interviews, we had lost a few of my aunts and uncles, and since then, we have lost several more and, with them, some of their stories and memories. For this I am deeply saddened. I wish I had begun this task earlier; however, I cannot go back so I will move forward.

In the pages ahead, I have factual information interspersed with my fictional dialogue and scenes, through which I have hope to achieve as close a resemblance to the events as possible. Obviously I was not yet born during this time, so I have had to use "poetic license" to fill in unknown information. Some names were made up as it's impossible to know the names of all those who were part of my great-grandmother's and my grandmother's lives.

I am extremely grateful to my mother and her siblings who willingly shared their memories with me and passed down stories they recalled. I am grateful to the Lord for placing me in a large family with our varied personalities, sense of humor, sense of duty to care for one another, and lessons on forgiveness for our human weaknesses. Life can never be perfect; however, I am thankful for the lessons of faith in a God and His Son, our Savior, who loves all of us in the midst of our sinfulness and wayward lives. We have the ability to rise above our circumstances with grace from our almighty Father.

As a famous, yet anonymous, quote says, "The secret to life is not what happens to you, it's what you do with what happens to you." As long as we learn from our mistakes, our trials and tribulations, then nothing is ever wasted or in vain. Often in looking back at the trials and triumphs of those who have come before us, we find a source of strength and understanding and even perhaps some answers about our own selves. I thank you for joining me on this journey.

Irene Cote Single, 2014

PROLOGUE

Snow swirled around Octave in the strongest storm he had witnessed in several years. Large flakes landed on his hat and jacket, coating him in white and molding him into the landscape around him. Fear gripped him as he searched his surroundings for something familiar. He had finished cutting as much wood as he could fit on his sled and hadn't noticed the intensity of the storm building around him. His focus was on getting wood to keep his family warm before that precious wood was buried too deep to access later. Now his eyelashes were covered with icy particles, and the path he had taken with his horse and sled had disappeared from view. It was dark and he couldn't make out which direction to turn. He hoped his dependable horse, Samson, would instinctively know.

Traveling between the trees, Samson plodded along with the heavy load and his passenger. Another eight inches of snow had fallen since Octave had left, which made the trek exasperatingly slow. His patience was running thin and he yanked on the reins and yelled to Samson above the sound of the howling wind. Octave envisioned his young wife pleading with him not to go out in this storm. Her pretty brown eyes showed fear that he hadn't seen since their wedding night.

He replayed their last conversation in his mind. Odile fervently pleaded with him, "Octave, it's too windy and it's snowing too hard. What if it strengthens? You won't be able to see two feet in front of you. Please don't go out in this storm. Wait until morning. We will be fine until then."

Octave had responded, "The wood will be buried deep and then I won't be able to get to it. What then, Odile? I must go out so we can keep the house and the children warm. I will be fine." He patted her cheek with his hand and smiled. His young children had looked at him with sad eyes as he'd bundled up to brace against the cold. ...

Suddenly the sled jolted and Octave realized Samson and the sled had picked up speed on the decline of a small hill. His heart quickened as he desperately held on to the reins and hollered to Samson. The poor horse seemed as anxious to get home as Octave was, but the heavy load behind him could barrel into him if he didn't keep the same pace. Drifts, six feet high in some places, hid the dangers beneath the snow, and Octave felt the right runner catch on something solid as Samson made a turn in the bend—or what looked like a bend. Octave wasn't sure.

As though in slow motion, Octave felt the sled rise as he slid down the left side and let go of the reins. His body slammed into the snow-covered ground as the load of wood shifted, causing the sled to tip over and land on Octave's legs, pinning him in place. He felt something else land beside him, and he reached out and touched the fabric. He pulled the wool blanket over him and yelled for help. He knew it was fruitless but he felt better doing it. No one else would be foolish enough to be outside in this storm.

His thoughts raced. *It's so cold. What am I going to do now? Lord, please help me. Send someone out to find me, Lord. How will Odile manage without me? I can't die out here in the cold. What a foolish man I am. I should have listened to her. She is wiser than I am. I don't even know where I am, how far away from home. How can anyone find me even if Odile could leave the house and get help? She can't leave four little children home alone, and she doesn't know which direction I went. I only told her I would be near the logging road, but then I went further than that and now ... I have no idea where I am.*

Octave yelled out to Samson and he heard his whinny, just barely. Samson couldn't move because he was still tied to the sled. Octave tried to dig the snow out from underneath himself with his gloved hands so he could slide out from the weight of the sled. The blizzard continued its fury around him as he struggled to get loose. Sharp pains shot through his legs as he tried to move them—he knew they were broken, but he didn't care. He had to get out. He had to get back to his family alive. If anything, his efforts helped him keep warm, kept the blood flowing.

Exhaustion from cutting the wood and then loading it onto the sled and from the injury to his legs only weakened him and he felt he was losing the battle. *Lord, I need a miracle. Please help me. Help my family.*

Octave had no idea how long he lay there cold, exhausted, praying. Again his thoughts went to his wife and in his mind he called out to her, *Odile, it's me. I don't know if you can hear me or feel me speaking to you. I am hurt badly. I am so sorry I didn't listen to your warning. Tell the children I am sorry and that I love them. I love you too. I need a miracle, but I don't know if I am going to get one or if my time here on earth is almost over. I am so cold and so tired, Odile. I have been lying here for what feels like hours and the snow continues to pile up. Please forgive me. ... So tired. ... So cold.* Octave felt a peace coming over him like he had never felt before.

*   *   *

No, no, Octave, don't go out in that storm, please. Please, Octave, it's too windy and it's snowing too hard. Come back, come back. Don't leave.

Odile awakened from her nightmare with sweat pouring down her face onto her nightgown. She gasped for air as her heart pounded in her chest. Rocking back and forth on her rocking chair, she held tightly to her bridal quilt. "Come back, come back!" she whispered into the darkness as the nightmare dreams became her reality. "Oh Lord, help Octave. Please. I know he is hurt; I can feel it. Please, Lord. Octave, hold on. I love you. Please. We need you. Hold on, Octave."

Chapter One

THE BEGINNING

Birds outside her bedroom window woke her with a start. Remembering what lay ahead this day, Odile's eyes filled with tears. Grudgingly she slipped out of the bed she shared with her sister, Elisa, and checked the time on the clock. *Six o'clock,* she thought as she sighed inwardly.

Odile softly made her way to her open window and glanced at the weeping willow tree. Its branches appeared lower than usual, matching her mood. Tears blinded her vision as her stomach knotted. Orange rays lifted over the horizon as she resisted the urge to run outside and climb that willow tree one last time.

Wringing her embroidered handkerchief between her fingers, her thoughts rushed back to two months prior. Papa and Mama had asked her to join them in the parlor after the young children were tucked in for the night. The house was quiet and Odile's heart quickened as she waited for Papa to speak. She pondered what she may have done wrong. She couldn't think of anything at that moment. Papa's dark brown eyes locked onto hers as he cleared his throat.

"There's something Mama and I would like to talk to you about. As you know, Mama and I have many mouths to feed and our crops are doing poorly because of the drought." His eyes shifted briefly to his wife before he continued. "You are old enough to get married now."

"*Oui*, Papa, I know, but I do not have a beau and—" Papa's hand went up, silencing her.

"I know, Odile. That is what we've come to talk to you about." He hesitated and took a deep breath. "Do you remember my friend, Octave Morneau?" Odile nodded. Her throat constricted. *No, he cannot mean him! Please, Lord, do something. Don't let Papa make me marry him!*

"Well, your mama and I have discussed this for a long time and decided you should marry Monsieur Morneau."

"But, Papa, he's so old." Her heart slammed in her chest and her hands became clammy. *This cannot be happening. I must be having a nightmare. Wake up, Odile!*

"His age doesn't matter. You are the eldest and we are counting on you. Octave's a fine man, Odile. He is successful, has a fine home, and will provide well for you. He has agreed to the arrangement. You'll see one day that it is for the best."

Odile dared not question Papa. She had hung her head to hide her tears.

Now, Odile shook the memory as she brushed her long, dark hair that was the color of a moonless night. *Mama always says, "If there is rain on a wedding day, the marriage will have many tears." There's not a cloud in the sky. A good sign, yes?* She swallowed and let out a quiet sigh, trying not to awaken her sister. *In less than two hours I'll be getting married. Oh, Lord, I am so afraid. Why would Papa arrange a forty-two-year-old husband for me when I am only fifteen?*

Kneeling beside the bed, she silently prayed, "Dear Lord, You know I am getting married today and how afraid I am. Please help me to trust in You. Take away my anger against Papa and Mama for not letting me choose my own husband. Help me to be a good wife and bless our future together. I ask for wisdom, strength, and courage to see me through this. *Merci, mon Dieu.*" Odile made the sign of the cross, stood up, and felt a little more at peace inside.

Although her future husband had never been married, she worried about their wedding night. *I must be strong and do the best I can. It'll work out for the best.* Her thoughts echoed her father's words. It didn't help relieve the jitters in her stomach.

At 8:00 a.m. on September 16, 1898, Odile Jalbert, dressed in a long, delicate, white wedding dress and a veil draped over her face, strolled beside her father, Arthur Jalbert, down the center aisle of the church. Moments later she stood, trembling, beside Octave Morneau in the Catholic church she had attended her entire life. Her sister, Elisa, as maid of honor, was on her left.

The church was set in the small village of Saint-Roch-des-Aulnais, in the county of L'islet, Province of Quebec, Canada. As she and Octave professed their vows before God, family, and friends, Odile said another little prayer, hoping it would calm her nervous stomach. Her petite five-foot-four-inch frame, a few inches shorter than Octave's, quivered. This was not how she had imagined her wedding day to be.

Octave was an only child, and Odile had several siblings. Today they would begin a new life together. After the wedding mass, a receiving line was formed and Odile blushed as family and friends said, "You look so beautiful" or "Congratulations" or "We'll be praying for you," or especially when her friends whispered things only she could hear. Her family welcomed Octave into their family and wished them both well. Afterward they all met at her parents' home for the reception, a full day of activities, music, and laughter. It was the longest day of her life. A part of her was thankful for the full day, while another part dreaded the alone time she and Octave would have later in the evening.

* * *

Grateful her mama and *grandmemere* taught her how to cook, sew, and keep a home in good order Odile met the responsibilities of being a new wife in a new home with greater ease than she had anticipated. It was hard work yet she was accustomed to it, being the eldest of seven children.

In October, Octave acquired help—including Odile's brothers, Arthur, Fabien, and Albert—to bring in the potato harvest, which they stored in large bins in the cold cellar. Prior to their wedding and in the few weeks following, Odile worked alongside her mother and sisters, Elisa and Alice, canning dozens of jars of string beans, pickled beets, dill pickles, tomatoes, and fruit. Although her parents had a large family and their crop wasn't as abundant as in the past, they provided several jars of canned goods to Odile and Octave as a wedding gift.

Odile mended Octave's shirts and socks and provided him with many flavorful stews, chowders, biscuits, and French bread. Octave's farmhouse lacked a feminine touch. One October morning as they ate breakfast diagonally across the table from each other, she bravely asked, "Octave, would you mind if I made new curtains for this kitchen?" She held her breath as she watched his eyes.

Octave wiped his mouth with a facecloth and looked around the kitchen as though noticing it for the first time. He ran his hand through his dark wavy hair. "Hmmm," he pondered, "I guess we could use some new ones. Don't know how long I've had these up, maybe fifteen years or more." Looking toward his young wife, he continued, "You go ahead and choose what you like. This is your home too." He smiled and patted her hand. Odile released her breath and smiled.

"*Merci*, Octave. I will look at some fabrics when we go to town in a couple of days." *Perhaps I can search for colors for the bedrooms and parlor just in case he lets me make new ones for those rooms too. One step at a time, Odile,* she scolded. They had been married two months and her

4

nervousness around him upset her. He had been kind, yet she wondered if she would ever get used to being married to someone close to her own father's age. She hoped someday she would love him as a wife should. She found it difficult to talk with him as they had such different interests and she had so little life experience.

A couple of days later they were in the general store. Octave needed feed for the animals, nails, and a hoe, as the wooden handle of his old one was broken. Odile strolled over to the rolls of fabric against the back wall. She unrolled one pattern, shook her head and rolled it back up; moved on to the next, studied it for a moment, rolled that one back up; and continued until she spotted a pattern she especially liked.

The little bell above the door jingled, signaling another customer. She heard the familiar voices of two of her friends and smiled. As she listened to their banter and giggles, tears formed in her eyes and she swallowed hard.

They can't see me crying. What is wrong with me? Just because they are still having fun, doing girly things, doesn't mean I should be unhappy. Oh good, they are talking with Madame Belanger. Relax, smile, all's well. Look at that pretty material; it's the softest blue I have ever seen. Those are the cutest little berries. It will make lovely curtains for the kitchen.

"Well, *bonjour* Odile. I didn't see you when we came in."

Odile spun around to see her friend, Suzette, her dark hair tied back in a bun and blue eyes flashing like diamonds. "Oh, *bonjour*, Suzette. I'm sorry I did not hear you come up behind me. I was trying to decide on fabric for curtains for the kitchen. How are you today?"

"Just fine, thank you," she replied. Then she added in a whisper, "How's married life treating you?"

In whispering tones Odile replied, "We are fine—just taking time to get used to each other. He's been a bachelor for so long and I am so young, that we think differently. He has been very kind, though."

"I can only imagine how difficult it must be for you with someone so, well"—Suzette looked over her shoulder to make sure no one, especially Octave, could hear—"old. Anytime you need to talk, I'll be here for you."

Odile felt the heat work its way up her neck to her face. She swallowed and responded, "Thank you, Suzette. That means a lot to me." In an effort to change such an intimate subject, she held up the blue fabric and asked, "What do you think of this for our kitchen?"

"It's lovely, Odile. You are a good seamstress so I am sure they will look perfect in your kitchen." She rested her right hand on Odile's left shoulder and squeezed slightly. Then Suzette gave her a hug. "Odile, I will continue to pray for you both. Now I need to get back to Jeannette and finish my shopping." Odile watched as Suzette meandered through the aisles and caught up with Jeannette who was still engaged in conversation with Madame Belanger. She turned her attention back to the fabric, but her mind wandered elsewhere.

Was it only a few months ago I was a young girl playing in the yard? Her mind's eye caught a glimpse of her siblings and herself climbing trees, swinging on the old rope swing, splashing in the pond, building snowmen and forts, laughing and running. It felt like a long-ago dream, yet it was only a few months ago that she was having so much fun.

Odile snapped herself back to her present-day situation, sighed, grabbed the roll of fabric, and asked Madame Belanger to cut the yardage she needed. Madame Belanger wrapped the fabric in brown paper, tied a string around it, and handed the package to Odile saying, "Thank you, Odile. You have a nice day, now." Octave came up beside her and paid for it, thanked the store owner, and carried the supplies to the wagon. Octave loaded their supplies into the wagon bed and assisted Odile onto the seat.

At home in the safety of her kitchen, Odile was haunted by all the "what if" questions as she measured and stitched the soft cotton fabric. What if she had been given the choice of who to marry, what if she had stood up to her father's demand, what if…

Oh stop it, Odile. It does no good whatsoever to play this over and over. It will just make you crazy, she scolded herself again. *I just have to accept my lot in life and move on. At least Octave has been good to me. There's no guarantee I would have had that with someone my own age. We are not struggling financially, so that is a blessing. That's what I need to do… count the blessings… not the what-ifs.*

A few days later Odile awakened at her usual time. As she swung her legs out of bed and stood up, she felt light-headed and flopped back on the bed. *What is going on? I've never been dizzy before.* She waited for the dizziness to subside before trying again, this time more slowly. Her stomach heaved and she rushed to the washbasin.

Thirty minutes passed and Octave came into the kitchen after milking the cows. No scent of bacon sizzling or eggs frying reached his nostrils so he called out for his wife. He took the stairs two at a time when he heard no response. He found Odile sitting on the floor in her nightgown, face pale, hair damp around the edges, clutching the edges of the washbasin.

Chapter Two

THE BABY

June 1899 was very warm, and this twentieth day was no exception. Sixteen-year-old Odile Morneau sifted flour to make biscuits in the kitchen when she felt a kick. "Oh! I felt that, Little One," she said, rubbing her abdomen. "Is today the day we get to meet?" Blending the biscuit mixture with her hands, another harder kick caused her to bend forward. "Oooohh. I think I had better have your papa get Madame Levesque," she whispered to her unborn child. She pulled a chair out and rested a few minutes.

Another contraction sent a spasm through her body as she stood and walked toward the front door. She yelled to Octave as she leaned against the porch rail. His head poked out the barn door. Seeing her face, he ran out of the barn toward her, stirring up dust in his path.

"What's wrong? Are you hurt? Is it time?" he asked when he approached the porch, breathless.

Her brow wet from sweat, she answered, "*Oui c'est temps.* Go get Madame Levesque quickly before the baby decides to come too fast." As Octave ran to the barn to hitch up the horse to the buggy, Odile waddled back inside the kitchen and moved the biscuits away from the oven, covering them with a clean cloth.

Someone else will have to finish those for me, she thought. Another spasm kicked from her abdomen and she bent forward, holding on to the

8

counter. "Oh, *mon Dieu*, help me." Grasping the railing, she slowly made her way up the stairs to their bedroom and lay on the bed.

Odile was taking short, quick breaths when the midwife rushed into the house a short time later with her medicine bag and clean towels. Octave had showed her to the upstairs bedroom. She quickly moved to the side of the bed to observe Odile and asked a few questions. Her gentle fingers checked the young girl's pulse as Odile told her when the contractions began. Sweat poured down Odile's face as the heat of the June day increased. Madame Levesque hurried to the kitchen and returned with a pitcher of water. With a wet facecloth she stroked Odile's forehead and arms to cool her down. She gave Odile a glass of water to quench her thirst.

"How long ago did you say the contractions began?" asked Madame Levesque as she pulled up a chair next to the bed.

"About an hour ago," whispered Odile.

"All right, you haven't broken your water yet so we have time. I will get some hot water going. When I return, I will see how far dilated you are. Breathe easy and continue short, quick breaths when you feel another contraction. I'll be right back." Madame Levesque stood up and exited the room.

Hours dragged on. Octave came in from the fields periodically to check on his wife, his brow furrowed. Worried it was taking so long, he left to fetch Odile's mother.

As the time drew near, Madame Levesque hurried into the kitchen to get the boiling water. She heard a carriage pull up and through the parted curtains she recognized Madame Jalbert, Odile's mother, climbing down from the carriage with her younger children in tow. Madame

Jalbert scooted the children toward the yard and rushed toward the front door.

Philomene (Lebel) Jalbert, was a slight woman with dark hair and a touch of grey, which was pulled back in a tight bun. She had a gentle smile and a calm presence about her. She had rushed over to help her eldest daughter as soon as she heard the happy news. When she entered through the screen door into the kitchen, she greeted the midwife.

"*Bonjour*, Madame Levesque, how are you doing today and how is my daughter?"

"I am fine, Madame Jalbert, and Odile is doing well. It won't be long now. Could you help me with these?" Handing towels and a clean tray with her medical tools to Madame Jalbert, Madame Levesque turned to lift the hot water pot off the woodstove and followed behind her across the wide pine floors and up the stairs.

The women stepped through the threshold of the room, and Odile's face brightened when she noticed her mother. Madame Jalbert laid the towels and tray on a nearby table. She held on to her daughter's hand and kissed her on the cheek.

"*Bonjour*, Mama," she whispered.

"*Bonjour, ma fille.*" (Hello, my girl). Philomene dipped a cloth into a nearby basin, squeezed out the cool water, and placed it back on Odile's forehead. "How are you feeling?"

"I... wish... it... were... over." Tears trickled down her cheeks.

Madame Levesque checked the progress and said, "It won't be long now, Odile. You're doing fine. You are a strong, young woman."

Breathing short, quick breaths, Odile replied in barely a whisper, "I… hope… so, Madame… Levesque. I… am… so… tired." Madame Levesque gently laid her hand on Odile's wrist, checking her pulse.

"Ooooh!" said Odile, grasping the sheet with tight fists, legs shaking. "I don't think I can do this. Mama, please help me."

"I am right here, Odile." Philomene, standing beside the bed, brushed her daughter's face with a cool cloth. She heard Octave pacing the wood planks of the porch below. "I think Octave is anxious. I hear him pacing." She chuckled.

Odile's contractions became more frequent as she tried valiantly to breathe short, quick breaths and held on tightly to the bedsheet.

Madame Levesque had the towel ready as she watched the progress of the baby. Finally she said, "Odile, it's time to push. That's it. … Again. You're doing well. Remember—small, easy breaths. That's it."

"*Aaaaaaahhh*," Odile screamed. Octave paced on the porch, pausing to look toward the upstairs window each time his wife screamed.

"Push again. I can see the head coming now. That's it. You are doing just fine. Push!" With one last scream, Odile pushed out the tiny baby. Madame Levesque caught the infant and smiled.

"Congratulations, Odile. You have a fine baby girl," pronounced the midwife as she slapped the baby's back, resulting in a loud wail. Madame Levesque cut the umbilical cord, cleaned the baby, and wrapped her in a tiny blanket before laying her in her mother's arms. Octave heard the wail of his firstborn child and entered through the screen door waiting for news, his nieces and nephews in his shadow.

"A tiny baby girl, you are," said Odile, smiling down at her little bundle, her hair soaked and matted. As Odile marveled at her tiny face, fingers, and toes, Madame Levesque cleaned her up, grabbed the soiled towels, and descended the stairs to tell Octave the good news. He whooped for joy, and the children beside him clapped.

Madame Jalbert looked lovingly upon her daughter and first grandchild and said, "Oh, Odile, she is so lovely. I could just eat her up. She reminds me of you when you were born."

Odile smiled down at the infant and replied, "You really think she looks like me?"

"*Oui*, she has a lot of your looks and some of Octave's. She is perfect. You had a lot of hair when you were born, too."

Madame Levesque stayed with the children while Octave removed his hat and washed his hands at the kitchen sink. Climbing the stairs two at a time, he came to a direct stop at the threshold to their bedroom.

Odile, smiling broadly, looked up when she heard Octave at the door. She said, "Come here and meet your daughter." Octave approached the bed slowly and bent down to peek at the little red face. "Isn't she beautiful? Look at her fingers and toes. They are so small."

"Yes, she is a beautiful girl. Look at all that hair." The baby had a head full of coal-black hair. To Odile, he asked, "How are you feeling, my dear?" He wiped her brow with the damp cloth.

"I am fine now, but it was quite painful for a while. I am so tired and hungry."

He chuckled. "You certainly earned the right to rest and eat if you wish."

"It has been hours since I ate. Oh, I forgot all about the biscuits I started making!" Octave and Madame Jalbert laughed.

"Don't you worry about the biscuits, Odile," said her mother. "I will take care of them. After I bring in the children for a peek, we will let you get some rest."

"*Merci*, Mama."

"You are most welcome."

Odile turned to Octave and asked, "Shall we name her Alice Marie as we had talked about?"

"Alice Marie is a fine name."

Looking down at her firstborn, she said, "Alice, say hello to your papa and your *memere*." Her tiny eyes flickered open and then closed as she went to sleep, content in her mama's arms. "She has had a rough day, poor little thing." Octave kissed Odile on her forehead, smoothing out her dark hair.

"You both should rest. I will go check on your brothers and sisters downstairs."

"*Merci*, Octave."

Octave glanced at his mother-in-law and said, "Thank you for being here, Madame Jalbert. I would be lost without you to help Odile."

"You are welcome, Octave. I will come with you." To Odile, she said, "I will be right back with the children."

Downstairs, Madame Levesque was cleaning up her medical tools and placing them back in her bag. She turned as Octave and Philomene entered the room. Philomene said, "Thank you for taking such good care of my daughter and granddaughter."

"You are welcome. I was happy to help. Your daughter is a strong girl. Are you going to stay for a while?"

"Yes, I am. I will take over for you. You have been here for hours and you must be tired."

"Yes, I am a bit tired. I will go then. Congratulations on being a *memere*. I will say good-bye to Odile, and I will be by tomorrow to check on her."

"*Merci*, Madame Levesque. I will see you then," said Philomene. Madame Levesque ascended the stairs while Philomene gathered Elisa, Albert, Arthur, Fabien, Alice, and Alfred to meet their niece.

They tiptoed up the stairs, peeked into the room in case the baby was sleeping, and whispered, "*Bonjour*." Still whispering, they offered to help with the household chores and caring for the baby. They quietly walked up to the bed, and Odile showed them their new niece. "This is Alice Marie, your niece." Their dark eyes opened wide, staring at the tiny infant in their sister's arms. Her sister, Alice, said, "Her name is Alice just like me?"

"Yes, just like you," said Odile.

A short time later, Octave hitched his horse to the wagon, and Madame Levesque climbed up into the seat. He grabbed the reins and they headed down the gravel road, wagon wheels sending dust in their wake.

When the two arrived at the home of Madame Levesque, she climbed down from the wagon and Octave called after her, "*Merci*, Madame Levesque, for taking good care of my wife and baby."

"You are welcome. I will be back to check on them tomorrow."

*   *   *

"She is so small," said Fabien.

"Babies are usually tiny when they are first born," said Odile as she chuckled.

Philomene said, "You let your sister and her baby rest, and you'll have plenty of time to help. Now you go on outside and play. Shoo!"

"But, Mama, can't we stay a few minutes?" they chimed.

"Not now, my dear ones. Now do as I say. It's a beautiful, warm day and the birds are calling your names. Mama will stay awhile to cook supper for Octave and Odile. Then we'll come back tomorrow. Elisa, you stay and help me in the kitchen." Philomene closed the door behind them. Through the open window she saw the children head for the wooden swing hanging from a limb of a large oak tree.

"Oh, how I wish I had half their energy," said Philomene, walking back to the bed. The room was plain, clean, and bright, with two windows facing east and one facing west allowing a nice breeze to cool the room. Pale yellow cotton curtains danced and floated against the sills. Odile had sewed new ones in the spring after convincing Octave they needed something brighter than dark blue. She had sewed new curtains for the parlor and the two other bedrooms as well.

"When you are on your feet, you'll be able to take a walk with Alice in the carriage. June is a perfect month to have a baby. You won't have to bundle her up heavily to keep her warm."

"I am anxious to go outside, smell the flowers, and check on the vegetables in the garden. Maybe the boys could help weed the gardens for me tomorrow," said Odile.

"That's a good idea. They wanted to help with something and I didn't know what. I'll bring them over in the morning. Papa will want to come by and see his first grandchild too. For now, I need to make supper for you and Octave. What would you like me to prepare?" asked Philomene.

"You'll find some leftover stew in the icebox to heat up along with some green beans and beets. Oh, and don't forget the unfinished biscuits. Octave will be back in about twenty minutes and he'll be very hungry."

"I am sure of that. There's some truth to that old saying that 'the way to a man's heart is through his stomach,'" said Philomene. Odile chuckled. "You rest while petite Alice is sleeping. I will put her right here in the cradle beside you."

Philomene descended to the kitchen. She found Elisa working the biscuit dough. Removing the green beans from the icebox, she placed them on the table. She lowered Odile's blue checkered apron over her head and tied the sash behind her back. Her olive complexion gave her the look of having a tan year round, and it darkened during the summer. Her dark brown eyes twinkled when she smiled, yet looked very serious and stern when she was not smiling. When she smiled, her small eyes narrowed almost to the point of being closed. A long thin nose and thin lips gave her face a serious look in contrast to Odile's rounder face, which gave her a youthful look.

Philomene snipped the ends of the green beans and snapped them in half while humming a tune quietly. She placed them on the woodstove in a saucepan with a little water. Then she took the jar of canned beets off the pantry shelf, twisted the cap, and pulled off the rubber lid. She gently poured the beets into a bowl to avoid a splash.

Philomene thought of how much her daughter had matured since her marriage. She recalled how frightened and angry Odile was before her wedding day and how she had wished she could convince her papa to cancel the arrangement. Now she saw how happy Odile was, and prayed all would be well.

Thirteen-year-old Elisa rolled out the dough with the rolling pin and pressed a glass upside down into the dough to make each biscuit. She turned slightly to speak with her mother and said, "The baby sure is a cute one, isn't she, Mama?"

"She sure is, Elisa. You are an aunt now. How do you feel about that?"

Elisa smiled wide and said, "I think I'm going to love it. She is so tiny though. I'd be afraid to break her." Philomene laughed softly.

"Most people think the same thing when a baby is born. Fortunately God makes them sturdier than that, although we still need to be very careful with them." She looked at the biscuits on the cookie sheet and said, "Those look very nice, Elisa. You did a great job. Let's get them in the oven now." Elisa opened the oven door and slid in the cookie sheet.

Madame Jalbert peeked out the kitchen window to check on her younger children who were now playing tag. *I'm still a mother with young children, fourteen and under, and now a grandmother, too. My little ones are young aunts and uncles. How fast the time flies,* she thought to herself.

She pulled out the leftover stew, spooned it out into another pot and placed it on the hot stove, stirring it frequently. While the food was warming, she took out the plates, mugs, forks, knives, and cloth napkins. Then she set a place for Octave at the table and one on a tray for Odile.

As the two worked side by side in the kitchen, Philomene remembered how busy Odile had been before Alice was born. She had baked a few loaves of bread and two raisin pies, washed and hung up the curtains, washed the wood floors, and mended Octave's socks. Philomene's mother used to tell her, "Before a woman gives birth, she gets her home in order just like a bird preparing her nest for her young." At that moment she realized the truth of that statement.

Philomene snuck up the stairs, peeked into the bedroom, and saw Odile and Alice sound asleep. *Good,* she thought, *they both need the rest.*

Since it was nearly five o'clock, she took the butter out of the icebox and placed it in the butter dish on the table next to the salt and pepper. Philomene heard horses' hooves clip-clopping on the dirt driveway as they neared the house. Philomene's sons called out, "*Bonjour,* Octave," as the horses came to a halt.

"*Bonjour, garcons.*" Octave pulled the buggy up to the barn, unhitched the horses, and led them into the barn.

The children ran behind him asking, "Can we brush him down, Octave, please?"

"Of course, you may. Remember to brush him like I showed you."

"We will," the boys said in unison as each one grabbed a brush from the tack room.

"Alice, let's go into the house and see how everyone is doing." The little girl skipped beside him as they headed to the porch.

Octave was still smiling when he entered the house a few moments later. "*Bonjour*, Octave," said his mother-in-law. "What are you smiling about?"

"The children couldn't wait to brush down Samson and Charlie. The excitement on their faces was priceless."

"Albert is almost fifteen and enjoys working on the farm. He's matured so much this past year. He doesn't seem to mind watching Elisa, Arthur, and Fabien, yet he is not quite sure how to handle the little ones," said Philomene.

"He's growing into a fine young man," said Octave. He scrubbed his hands at the black cast-iron sink. "Something smells good in here. What's for supper?"

"I warmed up the beef stew and cooked up some green beans. The biscuits are almost done, and the beets are on the table under the hand towel."

"Thank you for helping us. How are Odile and Alice doing?" he whispered as he glanced toward the staircase.

"They are doing fine. Why don't you go up and see them while I spoon out the stew."

Octave quietly walked upstairs and down the hall. He peeked into their bedroom and saw them quietly sleeping. He backed out slowly and quietly descended to the kitchen to eat his supper.

Madame Jalbert dished out the steaming stew into a bowl and put some beans on a small plate on the table. "Odile is content and feeling well. She's exhausted from the ten hours of labor, so it is good she is sleeping. Alice is so precious. She's been asleep the entire time. Newborn babies need a lot of sleep, and they eat every couple of hours. They'll probably be waking soon," she said.

"I'd better eat now while I have the chance." Octave's eyes twinkled.

"I need to get my own children home and fed. Will you be all right for a few hours? I can take care of the dishes when I come back."

"I'll be fine, Madame Jalbert. I was a bachelor for a good many years. I'll clean up after Odile eats her supper. You have your husband and children to tend to."

"*Merci*, Octave. I'll come by early tomorrow," said Mama. "Good night."

"Good night."

Philomene called to her children, who came running out of the barn. "It's time to go home. Are you hungry?"

"Yes! I'm starving," said Albert.

"Me, too," said Fabien.

The youngest two held their mother's hands, Alice on the left and Alfred on the right as Albert, Elisa, Arthur, and Fabien walked ahead. As they walked to their farm a mile down the road, they talked about their day and asked questions about baby Alice. Philomene couldn't get a word in edgewise.

Chapter Three

THE STORM

The next few years sped by as Odile gave birth to three more children: John, Alexandrine, and Alma. Alice was already an energetic, loving five-year-old with dark brown eyes that squinted almost shut when she smiled. Her long wavy hair was worn in braids twisted around her head.

Odile was now twenty-one years old and Octave was two years shy of fifty. His hair showed signs of grey near his temples. Young children around kept him feeling young yet exhausted.

The wind howled outside as Octave pushed the blue curtain aside to look out into the night. A winter blizzard had begun. Glancing at the dwindling pile of firewood stacked neatly by the woodstove, Octave made a decision.

"Odile, I need to go out and get some firewood in the woods before the snow gets too deep." He turned to look at his young wife.

"Oh no, Octave, the storm is too strong. Why don't you wait until the storm blows over and you can get some help from the neighbors," said Odile, concern rising in her voice.

"I will be all right. Don't worry. I will hitch up the sled, load what I need, and be back before the storm gets any stronger. I have to get the wood in so it can dry before we need it. If I leave it under the snow, it might freeze and I won't be able to budge it."

"Please, don't go. What if the storm gets worse?"

"I need to get wood, Odile. The pile is low, and if the storm goes all night I won't be able to get to it. What then? We need to keep the house warm for the children."

Feeling defeated, Odile said, "Please be careful, Octave. We will pray for you."

Octave gave his wife a quick hug and a peck on the cheek. Alice, John, and Alexandrine watched their papa put on his heavy boots, coat, hat, scarf, and gloves as they entered the kitchen.

"Papa, where are you going?" asked little Alice.

Octave picked her up, gave her a kiss on the nose, and said, "Papa is going to the woods to get some wood. Will you be a good girl for your mama while I'm gone?" He tickled her under the chin and she giggled.

"*Oui*, Papa, I'll be good," said Alice as he gently put her on the floor.

Four-year-old John looked up and asked, "Papa, can I come with you, please?"

Octave bent down and knelt in front of John. "Oh no, not this time, John. The storm is strong and not a place for little boys. Now give me a hug. Be sure you are good, too."

John lowered his head and murmured, "*Oui*, Papa."

Two-year-old Alexandrine grabbed her papa's leg and held on tight. Octave gently pried her tiny fingers off his leg and lifted her up to his chest. He gave her a kiss on her nose, and said, "Now, be a good girl too, all right?" She giggled and spoke words only her mother could understand.

Octave put her down, walked over to the high chair, and kissed baby Alma on the cheek. He tipped his hat to Odile and said good-bye, then pulled up his collar and braced himself against the wind.

In the barn Octave hitched Samson to the sled. He loaded his tools, shovel, and saw, placing them under the seat. Climbing aboard, he held the reins, clicked his tongue, and led Samson to the old logging road.

Odile busied herself with the usual nightly chores. She washed and dried the dishes and laid them on the shelves. Next, she cleaned the children's faces and hands, and sent the three eldest children to their rooms to change into warm pajamas.

With a damp cloth she scrubbed the high chair, rinsed the cloth at the sink, and returned to baby Alma. She cleaned her tiny hands, neck, face, and hair—food was stuck everywhere. She lifted the sweet baby out of the chair, gave her a soft squeeze, and gently set her on the floor. Alma waddled off to play.

Absently, Odile brewed a fresh pot of coffee for Octave's return and silently prayed for his safety. *He'll be chilled to the bone,* she thought to herself. Her thoughts wandered to their wedding day and how frightened she had felt. Octave had been nervous, too. He had held her gently while they spoke of their day and their hopes for the future. He was not a talkative person, but he'd been kind to her and their love had slowly grown over time.

Please come home soon, Octave, she thought, yet a feeling came over her that sent a shiver down her spine. A feeling of dread and sadness pressed upon her and she pondered what it meant. *Is Octave hurt? Or has something happened to Mama or Papa? Please, dear God, help whoever is in trouble,* she prayed.

The children broke into her tormented thoughts. Alice asked, "Mama, when's Papa coming home?" Odile turned to look at her four darling children, her heart bursting with love for them.

"It's dark and the snow is getting deep, Mama," said little John, peering out the living room window.

She took him by the hand and led him and the others to the couch and sat down. "Papa wants to fill the sled with wood, but because of the bad storm, it will take longer. He will need to drive the sled into the woods, cut down the small undergrowth in his way, shovel the snow off the fallen wood, and load up the sled. Let's pray for him."

They bowed their heads and Odile prayed, "Dear God, You know Papa is out in the storm and it is cold and he needs Your help to keep him safe. Please keep him safe for us and bring him home soon. Thank You, Father. Amen."

"Amen," said the children.

"It is getting late and we all need our rest, especially baby Alma," said Odile as she picked up Alma. "While I take Alma to bed, you three play quietly for a few minutes and then it will be time for you to go to bed, too."

Odile carried Alma upstairs to her crib. Removing the wet diaper, she took two cloth diapers out of the dresser, doubled them up for the night. Pinning the diaper securely, she slid a warm nightgown over the baby's tiny head. Alma rubbed her eyes and yawned. Odile kissed the infant on the cheek and tucked the blanket around her.

"Night-night, little one," said Odile. She descended the pine stairs to join the children in the living room.

"Can you tell us a story before bed, Mama?" asked Alice.

Odile picked up a hairbrush and gently brushed Alice's hair, beginning with the ends to remove the snarls. As she brushed her long, wavy hair, she said, "All right, let me see. Once upon a time there was a man whose name was Joseph, and he had a young wife named Mary. Mary loved God with all her heart, and God chose her to have His Son. Mary and Joseph had to travel very far with Mary sitting on a donkey. Joseph walked beside the donkey for miles and miles until they came to a tiny town called Bethlehem."

"Beth-e-hem!" said John. "That's a hard word."

"Try it slowly, John. Like this: Beth-le-hem." She began brushing Alexandrine's dark and shiny hair, which was now down to her shoulders.

"Beth-le-hem," said little John.

"That's right," said Odile. "When they arrived in Bethlehem, it was time for Mary's baby to come, but there were so many people in the town that there were no rooms left for them to stay in. The man at the inn said they could stay in the stable where his animals slept. Joseph took Mary and went to the stable. Mary's little boy was born that night and she named Him Jesus. She wrapped Him in old cloths to keep Him warm. Because He was God's child, too, the angels from heaven were so happy, they sang very loud. The angels told some shepherds in a field that the Son of God was just born in a stable, so the shepherds ran to Bethlehem to see the newborn baby.

"Mary and Joseph were surprised to see the shepherds. They listened to their story about the angels singing and telling them about God's Son being born that night. Then the shepherds knelt in front of the baby and thanked God."

"Did the cows see the baby too?" asked Alice.

"Oh yes, the cows, the goats, the donkeys, and whatever other animals were in the stable that night were able to see the baby. I think they may have been confused about people being in their stable, what do you think?"

"I bet they were, too," said Alice.

"I think so, too," said John. "What's a shepherd?"

"A shepherd is a person who watches over sheep and makes sure they are safe," said Odile. "Do you remember in church when Father Ouellette said that Jesus is a good shepherd?" The children nodded their heads, even Alexandrine, whose eyes were getting sleepy as she was cradled in her mother's arms.

"Well, Jesus is called a good shepherd because He takes care of all His sheep, which is all of us. We are like sheep to Him, and His job is to take care of us especially when things make us sad. Jesus lives in our hearts, and we can talk to Him any time we want."

"We can, even when we can't see Him?" asked Alice. She put her hand in front of her mouth, trying to suppress a huge yawn.

"Yes, you can, even though you cannot see Him. He can always see you and hear you. Now it is time for you to go to bed. I saw that big yawn and I can see Alexandrine's eyes drooping and John's too. So up you go. Let's be very quiet so we do not wake up Bebe Alma."

Odile picked up the sleepy Alexandrine and quietly climbed the stairs behind Alice and John. After she tucked them all under their warm quilts, she tiptoed into the room where Bebe was sleeping and rearranged her blanket. Quietly backing out of the room, she partially closed the door. Picking up the lantern, she descended to the kitchen. She pushed the curtain back and peered out the window into the storm. Strong gusts of wind plastered the snow against the windowpanes, and Octave was nowhere in sight.

Odile fetched the broom and swept the wide pine floor. After completing that task, she carried her sewing basket into the living room and mended her husband's shirts and the children's socks. Reaching into her apron pocket, she removed a tiny handkerchief with embroidery on the edges to wipe her brow. She remembered the day her mother gave her the matching pair on her wedding day. "I made these handkerchiefs for you so you'll remember how much I love you and that I'll always be near if you need me," she had said.

"Oh, Mama, how I wish you hadn't moved so far away," Odile whispered to herself.

Chapter Four

THE SEARCH

After her nightmares, Odile dozed off in the chair again having barely slept all night. The sounds of footsteps awakened her and when she moved, her neck felt stiff from sitting in the chair all night. John followed Alice into the room, their hair sticking out in all directions.

"Good morning, Mama. Did you sleep in the chair all night? Did Papa come home yet?" asked the children.

"No, I do not think Papa came home last night, but I will go upstairs to see."

"We already looked in your bedroom when we were looking for you, and he was not there," said Alice. Her tears were at the brink of flowing.

"I will check the barn then. You stay here and I will be right back. Try to be quiet while the little ones are sleeping."

"*Oui*, Mama."

Odile slipped on her boots, coat, muffs, and hat and opened the door. About ten inches of fresh snow had accumulated overnight with drifts as high as three feet in some places. Walking across the yard to the barn proved to be difficult with Odile's long skirts dragging heavily behind her. The sun was bright against the sparkling snow and she squinted to cut the glare. Unable to see any sign of a sled, she continued to the barn in case Octave was able to get in there, yet unable to get to the house.

Upon reaching the barn, Odile struggled to get the door open and barely squeezed herself in through the small opening. She called out Octave's name and searched the barn. The animals stirred, yet there wasn't any sign of a sled, Samson, or Octave. The cows needed to be milked, but she would have to do that after speaking to her children.

Trudging back to the house, soaking wet from the snow and out of breath, Odile entered the house. John and Alice looked expectantly at her with sad eyes.

"Your papa is not in the barn," she said, sounding out of breath. "He may have gone to a neighbor. I need to go back and milk the cows. When I return I will change into dry clothes and cook some breakfast and decide what to do next."

*   *   *

Hot oatmeal was dished into the bowls. The children quietly ate their breakfast while studying their mama. Sadness filled their small bodies. They sensed something was wrong. Mama usually hummed a song as she cooked their breakfast, yet today she was quiet. Minutes passed as they ate in silence. Finally, Odile spoke to John and Alice as though she just remembered they were in the room.

"Children, get on your coats and boots. I need you to walk over to Monsieur Gagnon's house. Ask him if he's seen your papa. If not, ask him to come right away."

"*Oui*, Mama, we can do that. We're big now," said John. He glanced over at Alice, who nodded in agreement.

"I know you are. That is why I asked you to do this for me. Let me get you bundled up warm. Then you can go."

Odile dressed John and Alice in their winter clothes and sent them out into the brilliant sun and snow. Monsieur Gagnon's home was roughly a half mile away. The children's progress was slow as they made their way through the sticky snow, staying close together. John, being a big boy, wanted to go first and clear the way for his sister, so she let him. His effort made it easier for her, considering her dress was almost drenched.

When they arrived at Monsieur Gagnon's home, they climbed the front steps onto the open porch and knocked. Monsieur Gagnon came to the door and looked down at two tired children. "Come in, children. What are you doing here so early in the morning? Is there something wrong?" He closed the door behind them.

Alice spoke up first. "Monsieur Gagnon, have you seen our papa? He did not come home last night."

"No, I have not seen him. Where did he go?"

"He went out to get wood in the storm. He didn't come home," said Alice, choking on her words. "Mama said if you didn't see Papa, come to our house right away."

"Oh my goodness. I'll get ready and go speak with your mama. You can ride on the sled with me." He turned to his wife as she entered the kitchen and told her why the children had come.

"I will take the children home and speak with Madame Morneau to find out what direction he went. Then I'll get some men to help me find him."

Madame Gagnon handed her husband his hat and scarf after he'd put on his boots and coat. She said, "Please be careful. The snow is deep. Do not rush or else you'll tip over the sled."

"I will be careful. Children, I'll get the horse and sled ready. Come outside once I am ready."

A short time later, Odile saw Monsieur Gagnon arrive with the children, and she stepped onto the porch to greet him, wrapping her shawl tightly around her shoulders. "Monsieur Gagnon, thank you for coming so quickly." She told the children to go in the house and remove their wet clothes and sit by the fireplace. Then she turned her attention to Monsieur Gagnon. "Octave left last night to get wood. He wanted to bring it in before it would be buried in the snow. I asked him not to go out in the storm, but he is a stubborn man and he left. I am terribly worried about him."

"Do you know which part of the woods he headed toward?"

"No, I do not know, only something about a logging road. He said it wouldn't take too long. Maybe he did not go far into the woods. Will you help find him?"

"Of course I will, Madame Morneau. I will get some men together and we will search for him. Do not worry, we will find him."

"*Merci*, Monsieur Gagnon." He tipped his hat, turned the sled around, and rode off, the snow spraying behind the runners.

"Mama, will Monsieur Gagnon find Papa?" asked Alice as her mother entered the house, her dark eyes showing worry beyond her five years. Odile removed her shawl and hung it on a peg and turned to face her daughter.

"*Oui, ma petite cherie*, Monsieur Gagnon and the other men will find your papa." She forced a smile and said, "Let's say another prayer."

The five sat at the table. Mama sat at the head of the table, baby Alma in the high chair on her right, and tiny Alexandrine on her left. Alice sat next to Alexandrine and John sat across the table. Odile bent her head and closed her eyes, and the three eldest children followed suit.

"*Bon Dieu*, You know where Papa is. We ask that You help the men find him quickly and bring him home to us. We thank You for our food and ask for Your strength. *Merci, mon Dieu.* Amen."

"Amen," repeated Alice, John, and Alexandrine. Little Alma giggled and kicked her feet, hitting the bottom of the tray.

"I will feed the two little ones their breakfast. Did you want a little more?" asked Mama.

John and Alice nodded their heads. Odile sprinkled a small amount of brown sugar in each of their bowls of oatmeal and poured some cream on top. The older children stirred the mixture and ate slowly. Mama fed Bebe, whose little legs and hands moved at a rapid pace. Several times her hands tried to take the spoon away from her mama, but Odile quickly pulled away and gently used her left hand to hold back the fast-moving fingers.

Once Odile finished feeding Bebe, she rinsed a washcloth and washed the squirming little girl's face and hands. Then she untied the bib, removed the tray and put Bebe on the floor to play. Odile ate her own breakfast while nagging fears of Octave pricked at her heart.

"Mama, we are done with our oatmeal and drank our milk. Can we play with Alma on the floor?" asked Alice.

Odile looked at the empty bowls and at her dear children's faces. A smile formed from her lips as she saw the white rings around their lips. "First, you must wash your faces. Then you may go play. Later on, you may go out and play in the snow and build a snowman or make snow angels."

"Yeah we can play in the snow!" cried John.

Chapter Five

THE RETURN

Three days later, Odile's hope had diminished. The men had returned each night without any sign of Octave. Suddenly she heard the distant sound of horses and sleds coming down the road. She wiped her floured hands on her apron, slipped into her coat, and stepped out onto the porch. She squinted to see if it was Octave's sled. Her heart pounded wildly as the riders approached. She recognized Monsieur Gagnon with several of the neighbors. They had Octave's horse and sled, but their faces looked somber.

Odile's heart continued to race, and thoughts ran amuck in her head. *It can't be good news,* she thought, *otherwise these men would look more cheerful. Oh dear Lord, be with me. Give me strength for whatever I am about to hear.* Monsieur Gagnon climbed off the sled and walked toward the porch. He removed his hat, held it in front of him, and twisted the edges.

"Madame Morneau, I am afraid we have some bad news. We found Octave a few hours ago lying on the ground under his sled. We are not sure what happened, but he froze to death. I am so sorry." He choked on those last words and looked down at his boots. With watery eyes he looked back up at Odile.

Odile's hand covered her mouth to stifle a cry as tears flowed down her face. She looked toward the house to make sure the children weren't listening by the window.

"Madame Morneau, your husband is on the sled. Monsieur Levesque and Monsieur Lamontagne left to fetch the priest and the doctor. Shall we put him in the barn until then?"

"*Oui*, Monsieur Gagnon, *merci.*"

"*Bien venue,* Madame." He tipped his hat and hurried toward the men.

Shivering, Odile entered the house to get her boots and told the children she would return in a few minutes. Without giving them a chance to ask questions, she closed the door and followed the men to the barn. Her neighbors shoveled the entrance in order to open the door wide enough for the sled.

Odile entered the barn and took a few steps toward the sled. She asked if she could look at Octave's face. Monsieur Gagnon pulled the blanket back as she moved closer. Startled at his still face, she gently touched his cold, blue cheek. Fresh tears rolled down her face. She turned away. Monsieur Gagnon covered Octave and gently led Odile by the elbow to sit on a bale of hay. The other men were discussing what ought to be done with his body, since it was winter and the ground was frozen.

Odile looked up at Monsieur Gagnon through wet eyes and asked, "How will I tell the children that their father is gone? They are so young to be without their papa." Her words came out in a whisper. He bent down on one knee in front of her.

"Father Ouellette and Dr. Bernard will be here shortly. Maybe Father Ouellette can go with you or I can if you wish," he said. "My wife, Antoinette, will also be here soon to help you as well."

She nodded and said, "*Merci.*"

The days passed in a blur for Odile. Her three older children clung to her skirts, as if afraid to lose her, and they cried often, especially at night. Her heart was broken. She needed to be strong and comforting for her dear ones, yet her energy was spent.

The neighboring women brought meals and offered to keep the children for a few days; however, the children would not leave her side. They barely ate anything those first few days. Odile had always enjoyed attending mass on Sunday mornings, but she could barely concentrate lately. The priest and the congregation meant well and offered sympathies and help and for that she was very grateful, yet she felt weighed down by her grief and the grief of her dear children.

Someone sent a telegram to her mama and papa in Maine in the United States informing them of the tragedy. Her aunts, uncles, and neighbors helped with the chores and the children throughout the remainder of the winter and into spring.

Chapter Six

A NEW COUNTRY

Alice, a lovely six-year-old girl, looked at her new surroundings. After leaving Canada, they traveled by train to their new home. This place called Sanford, Maine, was very different from the town where they had lived in Canada, and some of the people who lived there spoke differently too. It was impossible to understand what they were saying. She was glad she was with her mama, her sisters and brother, and her grandparents and great-grandparents who spoke French. Her mama said the people spoke English. Everyone she had known spoke French. Mama said they would have to learn to speak English, too, so they could speak with these people and the children could go to school.

In the center of town some of the houses were very close together and they didn't have barns or horses. Most people walked everywhere they wanted to go or someone with a buggy gave them a ride. Memere and Pepere Jalbert and Grandmemere and Grandpepere Lizotte also lived here. They left Canada a few years before, so Alice did not remember them well. She would get to know them soon since they would be living with her great-grandparents for a while.

Odile was determined to find work to help feed her four children. John, at age five, was a big eater. One day Odile said to her only son, "You must have a hollow leg and the food must travel down into your toes." John laughed so hard he rolled on the floor holding his stomach.

Alexandrine, at nearly four years old, liked to help around the house. Bebe Alma was not a baby anymore; however, being the youngest at one and a half, she was still called Bebe (Baby). She was a happy little girl.

Grandmemere and Grandpepere Lizotte's house, a tall two-and-a-half-story structure with lots of bedrooms, sat on a narrow road called Hammond Street about a quarter of a mile from the nearest mills. They rented rooms to people who came from Canada and needed a place to stay. Jobs were scarce in Quebec so many people ventured into the United States to find work at the newly opened mills owned by Mr. Goodall. People traveled by wagon, stagecoach, or train.

Because part of Maine connected with sections of Canada, unemployed men sought jobs closest to their homeland. The many mills in Sanford, in the southern part of the state, and in Lewiston, provided that opportunity. They needed workers, and they hired children as young as ten years old to work there as long as they continued their schooling at night.

Odile found a job at a nearby mill to help her parents and grandparents with the cost of taking in her family. Her mother agreed to care for the children while she worked. After selling her husband's farm in Canada, she paid the balances at the local merchants, and although they had some money to live on, she realized the funds would not last long with four other mouths to feed plus buying shoes and fabric to make clothing as they continued to grow. It was a huge adjustment for her from always living on a farm with open spaces, gardens, and farm animals to a crowded neighborhood in a busy mill town.

The older children went to school, learned to speak English, and made new friends with children in the neighborhood. Not wanting to lose their heritage, the family continued to speak in their native Canadian French while at home, especially since the Jalberts and Lizottes only spoke French.

Odile worked hard at the mill, arriving home hot and sweaty with the strong scent of lubricants permeating her clothing. The large brick mill buildings that were built along Mousam River had tall windows, filmy from dust and grime. The temperature inside the mills easily reached well over one hundred degrees during the summer months, and many people fainted from dehydration.

One day when she returned home, Philomene asked Odile how her day went. She responded, "Mama, it must have been 120 degrees in there today and two ladies fainted. They went home for the day, and we needed to work even harder to make up for their lost work. It's unbearably hot in there, and we have to drink a lot of water. We are on our feet all day, and I cannot wait to get these shoes off."

"Let me fix you some nice, cold lemonade. Would you like a slice of blueberry pie?"

"*Oui*, Mama, *merci*." Odile removed her shoes and wiggled her toes. "Oh, does that feel good." Her children ran in from playing in the tiny backyard, laughing and squealing.

"*Bonjour*, Mama," said Alice. "We've been playing hide-and-go-seek with our friends. You look tired, Mama. Are you all right?"

"I am tired. It was very hot in the mill. Which friends were you playing with today?" Odile took a long drink of lemonade, emptying half the glass and said, "Mmm, *c'est bon.*"

"We were playing with Jean-Paul and Celeste and Monique. They speak French too. Can we have some lemonade? We are so thirsty."

"I'll get it for them," said Philomene. "You rest for a bit. We will start supper in about an hour."

"*Merci*, Mama."

"*Bien venue.* Papa decided to paint the house since the paint is peeling in a lot of places and looks bad. He thought it would look nice in green." Philomene poured lemonade into small glasses for each of the children and placed them on the table. The children quickly drank them and held up their glasses for more.

"Green? Why green? Most of the houses in the area are white or yellow."

"That's exactly why. He doesn't want his to look like everyone else's," she said and chuckled.

"Oh, goodness," said Odile. "I suppose we won't have trouble finding our home from now on nor will anyone else. When does he plan on starting?"

"Tomorrow, if the weather is good. He will scrape the loose paint first, of course; then he will put on a white primer. When that is dry, he'll put on the final coat. It should take him a couple of weeks between working and rainy weather unless he gets help."

"Maybe on Saturday the children and I could help scrape the lower clapboards. I am not fond of getting up on a ladder. I'd just as soon leave that to the men."

"Me, too," said Philomene.

On Saturday morning, Odile, Alice, John, and Alexandrine scraped the lower boards as the sun warmed their bodies. As their clothes became drenched, they took a break on the front porch with fresh, homemade lemonade and blueberry muffins.

"Mama, do we have to go back and work some more?" asked John. "It's hot and I want to go play."

Odile searched the faces of her children and could tell they were exhausted. "All right, you can take a break for now. Later on I would like you to help for another hour and that will be enough for today."

"Yeah!" they screamed. "*Merci*, Mama." Quickly finishing their muffins and lemonade, they dashed down the front steps and ran around the house to the backyard.

"Oh, to be young again without any worries," Odile said with a sigh.

"Try being my age and see how that feels! You are still a spring chicken," said her mother.

"Most days I do not feel like a spring chicken. I feel old and frumpy. Like today." She leaned back on the rocking chair and sipped her cool drink.

"Odile, have you ever thought about marrying again? You are still so young."

"Oh goodness. Sometimes I wonder what it would be like to be married again, with someone younger than Octave…" She glanced at her mother to see her reaction. "But then I wonder who would want to marry a woman with four children. That's an awful lot to take on all at once."

Chapter Seven

ALICE BEGINS WORK

In 1912, at the young age of thirteen, Alice began work at Goodall Mills on High Street, located within walking distance of their home. It was hard work at the factory, especially for a young girl, working long hours on her feet. Many people, especially the children, suffered severe injuries; however, families needed the income in order to keep food on the table and pay their rent.

Alice, a smart girl, preferred to be in school during the day rather than working. One day she decided to approach her mother about her feelings.

"Mama, why can't I go to school during the day like the other children do?" she asked.

"Alice, we already talked about this. Our large family is poor and we need your help to buy food. Food and clothing costs have increased, and our family is growing. Plus we have to take care of this house. I wish you did not have to work and just have fun being a child, but we have no choice. I hope it will be for just a little while, but there is no way of knowing this," said Odile.

Alice nodded, feeling defeated. *No use arguing any more about it. Mama and Papa will not give in.*

It broke Odile's heart to send her little girl to a factory at such a young age. She had remarried a couple of years ago to Pierre Laprise, and had given him one child, Henry, and was expecting another. Pierre worked hard as a furniture salesman at S. B. Emery to provide for his ready-made and growing family. He had moved to Maine from Rhode Island after his mother died and his father moved the family to Sanford. Alice's income of a dollar a week would help their struggling family.

Hopefully things will be easier next year and I can send Alice to school during the day like John and Alexandrine. If not, I will have to send John to work too, Odile thought to herself. *Well, I cannot dwell on that right now,* she scolded herself. *We will somehow manage with the good Lord's help.*

Odile remembered the day she had announced to her family that a fine young man had asked her to marry him. Her parents knew she had an interest in Pierre as he had taken her places and had dinner with the family multiple times. However, when she made the announcement, their eyes widened and they couldn't speak. She laughed at their reaction and, as the shock wore off they congratulated her and asked so many questions at once. She had been a widow nearly five years.

Odile was personable, smiled often, and had learned to be strong in adversity. The young man had never been married and was willing to take on a wife and four children. Pierre was short of stature with a stocky build and dark hair. They moved to a home large enough to accommodate their growing family across the street from Odile's grandparents.

*   *   *

The years went by and Odile gave birth to three more children: Edgar, Yvonne, and Henedine. She had also lost two babies at birth. She was very protective of her family and although she was not a tall woman, she had a commanding presence. Her dark hair had touches of grey and was usually tied back in a bun. Giving birth to so many children added some weight to her once-small frame. Trials and tribulations strengthened her as she managed several children and a home. She prayed daily for her family and attended Holy Family Catholic Church a few blocks away. Her faith was passed on to her growing family, who knew that life could be tough and that they would need God to help them through.

Her firstborn children with Octave had slowly healed from the death of their father, but now it was as though he was forgotten except for the few photos she had stored in an album. They had been so very young that January, and she was grateful for the presence of the priest and her neighbors when she had to tell her children their father would no longer be with them and had gone to heaven. How it broke her heart to hear their cries those first few days and nights! Alma had cried too, although she was too young to really understand, but seeing her mother and siblings crying, she did also.

To compound the sadness, they had to leave their beloved village and country and travel hours to a strange place with a strange language knowing the possibility that they may never return to Canada. *Life strikes sudden blows, and we don't think we are strong enough to handle them until we walk through it and become stronger, more compassionate people in the process,* Odile thought.

Odile knew she would never have met Pierre if all of these events had never taken place, and she knew her Lord worked in very mysterious ways. Pierre was a good man even though, at times, he was stricter with Octave's children than with his own. The children needed to get used to him as well as he had to get used to having a ready-made family. He provided well for their needs, and he and Odile had more in common as they were much closer in age than her previous husband.

Odile prayed that Alice and all her children would someday find wonderful spouses and have dear families of their own. They were growing up so fast.... Her mother, Philomene, entered into the house and broke into her thoughts. She set aside the new what-ifs for another day.

Chapter Eight

NEWCOMER

Alice continued to work and attend school. She took piano lessons and learned to sew, knit, cook, and bake. Her lovely, shy smile caused her eyes to almost completely close and little crinkles to form at the corners, like her mother. She grew to about five feet four inches and her thick, dark, wavy hair fell down to her lower back. She had grown to become a lovely young lady at the age of nineteen.

Alice worked long hours at the mills during the week. On the weekend she visited her grandparents, the Jalberts; and great-grandparents, the Lizottes, as much as possible. One day, she strode across the street to visit her Great-grandmother Lizotte, who was still using her home as a boardinghouse. On that particular day, she spotted a handsome young man with a serious face and strong jawbone leaving the boardinghouse. He was about six feet tall and had tanned skin. His curly, dark hair was neatly trimmed.

Alice entered her great-grandmother's home a few moments later. She inquired who this stranger might be. "Memere? Who is that tall, young man who just left your house? I have never seen him before."

"Oh, him? He just came into town from Canada looking for work and needed a place to stay. Someone told him dat I rent rooms, so he came by to see if I had a room available. He is my new boarder. His name is Napoleon Alexandre and he is nineteen years old, just like you. It is a small world because he said he comes from Saint-Roch-des-Aulnaies,

45

just like us. You may not remember dat little town since you were a young child when your mama left to come here."

"No, I do not remember too much about it except that is where Papa died during that winter blizzard."

"Yes, that was a terrible ting dat happened, but good tings come out of bad situations, yes?" Alice found it endearing to hear her great-grandmother's pronunciation of some of the words. "Your mama married a man she loves, and we are all able to be together in the same town. How I missed all of you when we left Canada. It was very difficult to do, but dere was so little work at dat time," said Memere Lizotte.

"Has Monsieur Alexandre found a job?" asked Alice.

"*Oui*, he has found a job in one of de mills," said Memere Lizotte. "Maybe you will get a chance to meet him de next time you come by." She winked at her lovely granddaughter and said a prayer in her heart that she would find a suitable husband.

About a week later, Alice stopped by to visit her great-grandmother in hopes that a certain handsome young man would be there. She climbed the steps onto the open porch. Its roof slanted toward the road and the pitch of the floor was at a slight downward slant to allow the rain to run off. The porch floor was painted a light grey as were several in the neighborhood. Six pine chairs, two of which were rockers, painted a dark green, sat to the left of the door. A small wooden table, just large enough to hold drinks and refreshments, was set a couple of feet in from the railing. Many summer and fall evenings, the Lizottes and their boarders would sit outside and talk. Alice had often sat there listening to stories from her great-grandparents about the days in Canada.

Alice knocked gently on the door and let herself in as she had done so many times before. She called for Memere Lizotte. "Grandmemere are you here? Memere?" she continued as she walked down the hall, peeked into the sitting room and not finding her, let her nose lead her to the wonderful scents emanating from the kitchen. Grandmemere, dressed in a blue cotton dress that fell just below the knees, covered by a grey apron tied behind her back, stirred a huge cauldron of vegetable soup.

"There you are. I've been calling for you," said Alice as she kissed her on the cheek.

"*Bonjour*, Alice. I did not hear you coming. I am cooking soup for supper and I just took de bread out of de oven." She brushed away loose strands of grey hair with the back of her arm. "The boarders should be coming in about half an hour. Would you like to help set de table and slice de bread?"

"*Oui*, Memere, I'd love to help. How many people are you expecting tonight?"

"Well, dere are de tree boarders, Pepere and me, and you if you wish to stay for supper," said Memere Lizotte.

Alice retrieved six bowls and cups from the cupboard and set them on the table along with bread plates, spoons, knives, and cloth napkins at each setting. She reached into the cupboard for the salt and pepper and retrieved the homemade butter from the icebox. This she set on a plate in the center of the table. She sliced the warm bread and divided the bread into two baskets, placing one on each end of the table and covering them with a clean, red-checkered towel.

She heard a pair of work boots come in the front door and walk up the front staircase to the rooms above. She wondered if they belonged to the new boarder and a flush filled her cheeks. She looked over her shoulder to see if her great-grandmother had noticed, but she was busy at the woodstove checking on the soup.

"Is there anything else you need done, Memere?" Alice asked.

Her grandmother turned and scanned the table and said, "It looks like everything is ready, Alice. Thank you for helping. Dey should be coming down any minute. I see you will be joining us." She winked at Alice. "You can sit over here next to me after we serve the guests and Pepere." Memere always sat at the end of the table closest to the stove to better serve her guests.

A few minutes later, the upstairs doors opened and several pair of shoes and boots descended the staircase, and strolled down the hallway and into the kitchen. Pepere came in through the back door and washed his hands at the pump near the kitchen sink. Alice looked up at the tall man who entered the room and hardly noticed the other two boarders. Grandmemere introduced everyone, and Alice smiled shyly and said, "*Bonjour.*" The ladies ladled out bowls of soup to four hungry men. Once Grandmemere and Alice sat down, they bowed their heads, said grace, and hungrily dug into their meal.

The men spoke about their jobs, and Alice looked over at the young man at the far right side of the table. A couple of times she caught him looking at her as well and she blushed. It felt warm in the kitchen that evening.

She heard Napoleon talking about the farm his family owned in Saint-Roch and the large family he came from. He said something about leaving the farm to search for work in the United States after their Papa had died. He and his eldest brother, Joe, had argued and Napoleon decided to find other work to do. He had heard of other people from the Quebec province moving to Sanford, Maine, so he decided to give it a try. Joe traveled west toward Alberta, Canada.

Napoleon was strongly built with wide shoulders and muscled arms, slim in the waist, and long, lean legs. He wasn't afraid of hard work and enjoyed working outside in the fields and woods. Besides farm work he also logged in the woods in Canada. His stern face brightened to a cheerful one when he smiled, and Alice's heart skipped a beat.

After supper was over, Alice helped Grandmemere wash and dry the dishes. Alice's thoughts were on the young man, and she wondered when she would see him again.

Chapter Nine

BIRTHDAY

Several weeks later, Alice celebrated her twentieth birthday on June 20. Her mother recalled the warm day when her first child had entered the world. "You were so tiny. Your papa and I marveled at your tiny toes and fingers. Sometimes it feels like only yesterday, and other times it feels so very long ago. So much has happened since that day," said Odile wistfully.

"Were you afraid to be a mama at sixteen years old?" Alice asked.

"Oh, *oui*, I was very afraid. When the pains began, I wasn't sure at first what was happening, but then I remembered my mama telling me a little bit about what to expect. It's a good thing she did, otherwise I might have panicked." She chuckled. "The labor lasted for hours and the day was very warm. I could hear your papa pacing on the floorboards on the porch toward the end. I think he was just as scared as I was."

Odile smiled as her mind wandered to that day twenty years ago. She was caring for another human being and she was barely out of childhood herself, and the thought had overwhelmed her. She was grateful her mama came by each day for the first few weeks to help even though she had several young children at home. Even the midwife returned as promised to make sure all was well. Odile had slept very little those first few weeks as the baby needed to be nursed every two hours.

"Mama, did you hear what I asked?" Alice said, breaking into her mother's thoughts.

"I'm sorry, what was it you asked? I was thinking back to the day you were born."

"I just wanted to know if you'd met Grandmemere's newest boarder yet."

"No, not yet, but I have seen him walking by. He is a handsome one." She winked at Alice. Alice blushed.

*   *   *

One Saturday on a hot July afternoon, Alice stopped to visit her great-grandparents at the boardinghouse. As she approached the home, she noticed Napoleon sitting on the front porch speaking with her grandparents. "*Bonjour*, Memere and Pepere, how are you today?" Alice bent down and kissed her great-grandmother on the cheek.

"*Tres bien, merci, et vous?*" asked Memere Lizotte. Pepere nodded and winked at her.

"I am happy to hear you are well. I am well, too, thank you." Alice turned toward the gentleman sitting beside her grandmother and said, "*Bonjour*, Monsieur Alexandre."

"*Bonjour*, Mademoiselle Morneau." He tipped his head and looked at her with his deep hazel eyes as though he were studying a book. She felt her face flush.

"How did your job at de mills go dis week, Alice? You look worn out," said Memere. "The Goodalls shouldn't have young ladies work such long days."

"It was a difficult week mostly because it is so hot in there. A couple of older women passed out from the heat, and the doctor was called in. He checked their pulses and temperatures, gave them water, and sent them home for a few days of rest. Our supervisors brought us some extra water after that."

"That's why I prefer outdoor work," said Napoleon. "Even though it gets hot, at least the air is moving most of the time. But indoors with the heat of the machines, it gets too stuffy. I hope to find a different job than working in the mills."

"Yes, dat's true," said Pepere. "I remember working on days when it was 95 degrees outside and over 120 degrees inside. Phew!" He wiped his brow and shook his hand, pretending to shake off the sweat, and continued, "*C'est ta chaud, mon doux.*" (My back, it was hot!) It was a strange expression when translated into English, but most French people said it often. "Many people passed out den, too, and were sent to de doctor or de hospital. It is not fun working under dose conditions. I am sorry, Alice, dat you have to work dere. It is not a place for a smart young lady like you."

"We need the money at home, Pepere, so I need to do this for now until I can find something better. With Mama's little children at home, the times are even harder. I will be all right, though."

"I know you will. You are strong, even though you are a small one. You have never been afraid of work."

"Maybe you will get married someday and your husband can take care of you," said Memere with that twinkle in her eye.

"Oh, Memere, I do not see that happening too soon." Alice looked down at her hands and twisted her handkerchief on her lap.

"Don't you have a beau, Mademoiselle Morneau?" the boarder asked. Alice looked up at the stranger with a bit of embarrassment that he would ask her such a question when they had only met once! Her grandparents looked as stunned as she felt.

"No, right now I do not have a beau, Monsieur Alexandre."

His large hand scratched at his day-old beard. "Well then maybe we can go for a little drive sometime if that's all right with you."

Alice's dark brown eyes widened. *This man is not shy,* she thought. She looked at her grandparents who only shrugged their shoulders and smiled. Then she turned to the handsome boarder and replied in her sweet, gentle voice, "Perhaps we could." She blushed again when he smiled at her.

*　*　*

A few weeks later, Napoleon drove a buggy to Alice's home just a street away. His long legs took two steps at a time onto the porch and he knocked, louder than he intended. A stout woman in her late thirties opened the front door and looked at him through the screen door. "Yes, can I help you?" she asked.

He cleared his throat and said, "I am Napoleon Alexandre. I am boarding at Monsieur and Madame Lizottes', and I wondered if Mademoiselle Morneau is home."

"Yes, she is. I am her mother, Madame Laprise. Won't you come in, please?" She swung open the screen door for the tall, young man. *Is this the young man Alice spoke about?* she asked herself. *Oh yes, I remember seeing him at Memere and Pepere's.*

He removed his hat and said, "*Merci*, Madame Laprise." She led him to the living room and went in search of Alice. When she found her in the tiny backyard, she told her a young man was looking to speak with her. Alice stood up in surprise. Her grandmother, Philomene, sat on a rocker just outside the back door, knitting a baby sweater. She looked up at her eldest grandchild with sincere delight.

"He said his name is Napoleon Alexandre. Is this the young man you spoke about briefly a few weeks ago?" asked Odile.

"*Oui*, Mama. That is him. He said that he would take me on a little drive with him sometime if that was all right. I just didn't expect him to actually do it."

"Well, of course it is all right. You are twenty years old and a mature young lady. He's in the living room, so let's not keep him waiting."

"I am nervous, Mama." Her mother wrapped her arm around her daughter's shoulders and gave her a quick hug.

"It will be all right. He seems like a fine young man. You go on and have a good time."

They walked back into the house together. Napoleon stood as they entered the living room. "*Bonjour*, Mademoiselle Morneau," he said.

"*Bonjour*, Monsieur Alexandre," Alice said shyly. "I am surprised to see you here."

Her mother turned to their guest and asked, "Would you like a glass of lemonade?"

"*Non, merci*, Madame. I wondered if it would be all right to take your daughter for a ride for a couple of hours, if she wants to."

"It is fine with me if Alice wants to. Do you wish to go, Alice?"

"*Oui*, Mama." She looked down at her feet, not daring to look him in the eyes. "Shall I get a sweater, Mama?" Any excuse to leave the room for a few minutes to gain her composure was what she needed.

"*Oui*, take a sweater with you just in case it gets cooler." Alice headed upstairs to her room to retrieve her sweater, her stomach all jittery with anticipation.

"Madame Laprise, I will drive slowly. I thought we would go to the pond downtown and then toward Springvale. I will be sure to have her back in less than two hours," said Napoleon.

"Good. You take good care of my daughter. She is a special girl."

"*Oui*, Madame, I will."

Alice came downstairs with her sweater draped over her left arm, her face red and flushed. "I am ready to go."

"*Merci*, Madame Laprise," he said as he opened the front door for Alice.

"*Bien venue,* Monsieur Alexandre. I will see you in a couple of hours. Have fun, Alice."

"Bye, Mama. *Merci*," said Alice.

It was a beautiful, sunny, July day with a slight breeze from the east. Napoleon helped Alice into the buggy, walked around to the other side, and climbed up beside her.

"How are you today, Mademoiselle Morneau?"

"I am well, thank you, and yourself?"

"Very well, thank you. You may call me Napoleon or Poli (pronounced Polee), as my friends do. I thought it would be a nice day to drive over to the pond downtown and then to Springvale. How does that sound to you?"

"Yes, that would be fine. You may call me Alice. It is a beautiful day for a drive. Where did you get the buggy?"

"From a friend of mine. His name is Gilles. He said, 'Take it for the afternoon if you wish,' so I said, 'Thank you, I will.'"

"I haven't been toward Springvale in a very long time. Have you been there before, Napoleon?"

"Only once. Some men I know needed to get supplies and asked me to come along. It is a beautiful drive, lots of trees and flowers." The buggy rattled along the dirt roads, and in about ten minutes they were at the pond. Napoleon reined in the horse and pushed the brake. He jumped down and went around the buggy to help Alice down.

Once they were standing on the grass beside the pond, he asked, "What is the name of this pond?"

"It is called Number One Pond. Funny name isn't it? Someone said it has something to do with the Mousam River running into it. When it was dammed up to make a pond for the mills, they named it Number One, since it was the first pond created by the river flow."

For a short while they walked along the grassy edges watching the ducks bathing themselves in the pond. The sky was a clear blue. Along the horizon there were mounds of white puffy clouds that looked like children rolling around under blankets. Alice smiled at the thought.

She remembered a time long ago when she and her younger siblings had all climbed into the same bed, hiding from their mama, thinking that she could not see them since they could not see her. All the while, they didn't stop wiggling and giggling.

Mama pretended she did not know where they were. She kept calling for them, "Alice, John, Alexandrine, Bebe, where are you children? Are you playing hide-and-seek on Mama?" Her footsteps went in one room, then another, and another until finally she came into the bedroom where they were hiding.

"I wonder where those children are hiding. Are they under the bed? No. No one under here. Are they in the closet?" The door squeaked open. "No, not here. Hmmm, I wonder where they could be?" The lumps under the blankets were moving up and down, and she could hear quiet whispers of "Shhh, be quiet."

Next thing the children heard was their mama moving closer to the bed. "I wonder if they are over here," she said. *"Une couvat, deux couvat, troi couvats."* Mama was counting each blanket as she lifted them back, and the closer she got to the lumps, the more wiggling and giggling could be heard. When she got to the last blanket, she pulled it up quickly and said, *"Je te mange!"* (I am going to eat you!) The children screamed hysterically, laughing and kicking their little legs. Mama tickled their little bodies and fell in beside them. The children climbed on top of her, messing up her hair and tickling her.

"Alice? Alice?" Napoleon's voice snapped her out of her reverie. "What were you thinking about? You were a million miles away."

"Oh, I am so sorry. I was just thinking of something back when I was a little girl."

"Do you wish to share it with me?"

Alice relayed her story and he chuckled. "I can just picture four little children under a blanket. My four brothers and three sisters and I used to hide like that too. We always thought we were so clever." Napoleon's eyes twinkled and his thoughts went back years. Growing up on a farm with lots of brothers and sisters was fun, especially when they played games and built things from scraps of wood and nails. Of course, there were many chores to do too, but they would get those done early in the morning so they'd have time to play.

He realized how much he really missed his family. He was the only one who left Canada after his fight with Joe, his oldest brother. He couldn't write home telling them where he was without help from someone who could write. He had to impose on others to write letters that he dictated and read the letters that came in reply. It was rather embarrassing. Although he had kept busy finding a job and then working, it was still hard to be so far away from home. He missed his mother, brothers Joe, Eugene, David and Louie, and sisters Juliette, Adine and Diane, and the farm terribly.

"Napoleon!" Alice interrupted his thoughts. "Now it is your turn to be a million miles away."

"Yes, I too was thinking back to my younger days and my family back in Canada."

"I imagine you miss them very much," she said. "It was hard for me as a young girl to leave Canada, but now we have been here many years. Could you tell me a little about St. Roch? Grandmemere says you came from the same village as me. I do not remember much about it since we left when I was only six."

"Your grandmemere said your papa died when you were young. What happened?" They were walking side by side along the gravel road near the pond, enjoying the beauty around them.

"When I was only five years old, Papa went out one night in a snowstorm. He told Mama he needed to get the firewood out of the woods before it got buried in snow. She told him it was too dangerous to go out in blizzard conditions, but he was stubborn and had to go. When he didn't return by morning, Mama sent my brother John and me to a neighbor to see if he'd seen Papa. He hadn't, but promised to get some men together to search for him. On the third day, they finally found him frozen to death under the sled. They weren't sure what had happened; however, they felt the sled must have tipped and he lost his balance and landed underneath it and was trapped." Alice wiped a tear from her eye.

"We missed him terribly. It was a difficult winter having no papa. Our family and neighbors helped out a lot. They brought plenty of food and helped keep our wood supplied so we would be warm. It was very hard on John. He was the only boy and only four years old. Alexandrine was little and Alma was just a baby." Alice turned to look up into Napoleon's face and saw sadness in his eyes.

"I am sorry you lost your papa at such a young age. I can't imagine what it must have felt like. I lost my papa just a year ago and that was hard on all of us, but we were grown. Your mama must be a strong woman to have gone through all of that at her young age."

"Yes, she was a widow at twenty-one with four young children to care for. When we moved to Sanford, it was another adjustment we needed to make. That's one of the reasons I had to go to work at a young age. We needed money to put food on the table and, being the eldest, it was my responsibility to help out. I would have preferred going to school, though I had no choice." Alice sighed.

A short while later they walked back to the buggy. The ride to Springvale was pleasant and a soft breeze blew in from the east. Alice put her sweater on for the return trip. As promised, Napoleon had her home in less than two hours. He walked her to the door and she said, "Thank you, Napoleon, for a lovely ride. I had a good time."

"You are welcome, Alice. I had a good time, too. Would you like to do it again sometime?"

"Yes," she said shyly, "I would like that. Well, good-bye."

"Good-bye."

Alice opened the door, turned, and waved as Napoleon rode off. Her mother and grandmother were drinking tea at the kitchen table, anxiously awaiting news of her date. Alice removed her sweater and hung it on the hook in the hall.

"*Bonjour*, Mama and Memere," she said. She took a seat at the table opposite the women.

"*Bonjour*, Alice. How did it go today with Monsieur Alexandre?" asked her mama, grinning from ear to ear.

"We had a very nice time. We talked about Canada and our childhood, and about you, Mama, becoming a young widow. Grandmemere had told him that Papa had died years ago so he asked about it. He was very kind and polite."

"Sounds like you had a nice time. I am glad. You need to get out more with young people," said Odile.

"I agree," said Memere Jalbert. "You work too many hours during the week, so it is good for you to have some fun on the weekends and be with people your own age. Did you make any plans to get together again with Monsieur Alexandre?"

"He asked if I would like to do it again sometime, and I said yes." Alice's face turned a deep red. She bent her face and pretended to straighten the edge of the tablecloth.

"Well, that is nice. Maybe if you get married you won't have to work in the mills anymore," said Odile.

"Oh, Mama, we only had one date and already you are talking marriage!"

"Why not? You turned twenty last month. Why shouldn't I think of marriage for my first born?"

"Well, because it is a bit soon to think that way. We may find we are not meant for each other. I want to be sure before I rush into anything, Mama."

"I did not mean you would get married tomorrow, Alice," she teased.

Memere Jalbert watched and listened to her daughter and first grandchild speaking like best friends. She couldn't believe that Alice was twenty—a lovely, mature young woman. *Wasn't it just last week that she was born on that warm June day? How time flies the older you get,* she mused to herself.

She reached across the table and touched the top of Alice's right hand and said, "You are a very special young lady, and I know your mama wants what is best for you as do I. You take all the time you need to be sure you make the right decision about de man you will spend de rest of your life with." She gave Alice's hand a gentle squeeze.

"*Merci*, Memere. I know you both want what's best for me. Believe me I will not hurry into a decision as important as marriage. Monsieur Alexandre wants me to call him Napoleon or Poli, his nickname. He comes from a large family, and they are all still in Canada. He misses them very much. However, he wants to try to make it on his own here since one of his older brothers is running the family farm now. I think he is a very determined young man."

"Grandmemere Lizotte said he is a hard worker and always pays his rent on time," said Memere Jalbert.

"He said he enjoys living there, and that Grandmemere is a good cook," Alice said. "A good meal is important to a man, I guess." She shook her head back and forth for emphasis. They talked for a while, sipped their tea, and made plans for Sunday dinner. Alice pondered her next encounter with Poli. A short while later, Alexandrine and Alma returned home from a visit with friends. John was out with his male friends and was due back for supper. The youngest were outside playing with the neighbors. Alice felt in her heart that things were about to change.

Chapter Ten

ALICE AND NAPOLEON

The following Sunday afternoon, Alice and Poli walked around the neighborhood. Her mother watched as they turned the corner a hundred feet away, and she chuckled at the difference in height, her little girl at five feet four inches and Poli at over six feet. *How strange life is. We lived in the same village in Quebec, yet I never met the Alexandre family. Then we travel all this distance to southern Maine, and Alice meets a boy from back home. I wonder if the Lord is up to something.*

Alice and Poli returned an hour later and ascended the front porch steps. "Would you like some lemonade, Poli?" Alice asked.

"Yes, I am very thirsty, thank you." Alice smiled and opened the screen door, returning a few moments later with two glasses of cold lemonade. She handed one to Poli and sat on a chair beside him. As they sipped their cold drinks, they laughed about stories they had heard at work during the week. Alice found him to be very clever and enjoyed his stories. She decided she had better stay on her guard—from the stories he was telling her, he was quite a prankster. Her heart skipped and fluttered every time he smiled at her.

Alice's stepfather, Pierre Laprise, had been visiting a friend a couple of blocks away and strolled down the sidewalk toward his home. He had not yet met the young man who was keeping his eldest stepdaughter's interest in the past few weeks. Alice spotted him turning the corner toward home, a couple hundred feet away, and her stomach knotted. She realized she wanted Pierre Laprise's approval of her new friend and was unsure how he would react toward him. She stood up as he approached the staircase and said, "*Bonjour*, Papa."

Pierre Laprise glanced up at the sound of her voice and ascended the front steps and said, "*Bonjour*, Alice."

Poli stood to her left and extended his hand as Alice introduced her stepfather to her friend. "Papa, I would like you to meet Napoleon Alexandre. Napoleon, this is my father, Pierre Laprise."

They shook hands and Pierre said, "Good to meet you, Napoleon. I am sorry I have missed you the past couple of times you have been here to see my daughter."

"Good to meet you, too, sir. Please call me Poli. I would have liked to ask your permission to see Alice. Madame Laprise said it would be all right."

"Yes, of course, of course, it is fine. Let's sit down. No need to stand in the hot sun."

Pierre lifted a chair and moved it closer to where Alice and Napoleon had been seated. Odile pushed the screen door open carrying a glass of lemonade for her husband and a pitcher to refill Alice's and Napoleon's glasses.

"*Merci*, Odile," said Pierre to his wife. "How did you know I needed a cold drink?" He winked and gave her a silly grin, and she knew her husband was going to give their guest the third-degree questioning, just to test him. She rolled her eyes at him, and it wasn't lost on Napoleon.

"Why don't you join us, Odile. I'll get you a chair." Pierre stood and moved his chair over for her to sit. Then he retrieved another and set it down beside her. Alice knew something was cooking with her stepfather and hoped he wouldn't be too hard on Poli and scare him off. Odile poured some lemonade for herself and set the pitcher on the floor in the shady area. Her young children's laughter and screeches from the backyard could be heard easily with the doors and windows open.

"What type of work do you do, Napoleon?" asked Pierre.

Poli crossed his right leg onto his left knee and rested his right hand on his shin. He glanced over to Alice on his right and back to her stepfather. "Well, sir, I work in the Goodall Mills right now but I like to work with wood and I like farming. I prefer working outside. The scents from a farm and the fresh air are better than being in a stuffy mill. But since I have been here just a short time, it was the first job I was able to find."

Pierre smiled and said, "My wife used to work in the mills, and Alice has been working there about six years. They have shared stories about the heat and noise of the mills. I can see why you would not like it. What are your plans for the future? Do you wish to move back to Canada or will you be staying here?"

"One of my older brothers is running the family farm, so there is no place for me there. We don't agree on how to manage it, so I expect to stay here in Maine. I would like to buy land, log wood off of it, and resell it later. Sometime I would like to buy my own farm or land and build my own home."

Pierre Laprise scratched his chin and sipped some lemonade before asking his next question. "Do you send money home to help the family?"

"No, most of the family is grown now and my older brothers and sisters take care of my mother. I plan on saving as much as I can for my own farm."

Pierre asked many questions, and Napoleon met the challenge straight on. Sometimes they laughed and other times they were serious. Pierre eventually gave his permission allowing Napoleon to call on Alice as often as he would like as long as Alice agreed and it did not interfere with her work at the mills and home.

Chapter Eleven

FAMILY GATHERINGS

Poli joined Alice; her parents; her brother, John; and sisters, Alexandrine and Alma for a game of cards. Since the group was large, they separated into two groups after her young half siblings went outside to play or down for a nap. Outside the kitchen windows, stunning red, orange, and yellow leaves hung on the maple and oak trees as autumn temperatures cooled and fresh breezes lifted the leaves and sent them floating down to the ground. Alice watched them as she waited for her turn.

She marveled at how some leaves floated back and forth gently to the ground, others spiraled quickly, while still others glided along almost afraid of touching the ground. Alice silently gazed at the dance outside the window. She contemplated how each autumn some oak leaves hung on all winter, only to be released from their bondage in the spring when fresh buds pushed them off. *How lonely it must be for those leaves all alone on the new grass,* she thought, *while the other leaves had nurtured the roots and the ground all winter long.*

"Alice, it's your turn," said her mother.

"Sorry, I was just watching the beautiful leaves outside." She placed her card on the table and the game continued. Chatter filled the air around her as she reflected on seasons past and what her future held. Glancing across the table, her eyes connected with Poli and her heart fluttered. He winked and she smiled. Observing her family, she noticed how different their expressions were as they mulled over which card to throw down. Her dad scratched his chin, her mother twisted a button on her dress, Alexandrine furrowed her brow in concentration, John moved his thumb up and down along his jaw, and Alma studied her cards close to her face. Alice chuckled inwardly.

The years have passed so quickly, Alice thought. *Mama is still having babies, and maybe in a couple of years I will have one of my own. It will be strange having children around the same age as my half- brothers and half- sisters.*

The card game ended and Odile pushed her chair back and said, "Is anyone ready for an afternoon snack and some coffee or tea?"

A resounding yes echoed through the room. Alice and Alexandrine stood up and followed their mother to the other side of the kitchen as the others stood to stretch their legs. Coffee percolated as Alice put the kettle on the woodstove for tea.

Alexandrine retrieved banana bread stored in the pantry, and Odile gathered up dessert plates and cups. Alice took out the cream and sugar and placed them on a tray.

"I like playing cards, don't you, Alice?" asked Alexandrine. Alexandrine cut the bread into slices and laid them on a plate, placing a container of butter beside it.

"Of course I do. It's a nice way to spend an afternoon," said Alice.

"Your mind did not seem to be with us during that last game. Are you feeling all right?"

"I am fine. I was enjoying seeing the leaves blowing off the trees. It is so pretty this time of year. It's too bad the season is so short. Winter will be here before we know it."

"That's true," said Odile. "It seems as though we just had winter, and here it is October already. Where does the time go?" She rubbed her swollen belly.

Alice turned the kettle off and filled three cups while Alexandrine poured coffee for the men and boys.

"Everything's ready," said Alice. "Let's go feed the hungry ones." The girls carefully picked up the trays before their mother had the chance, noticing she was getting tired.

"You go first, Mama. We'll be right behind you."

"*Merci*, Alexandrine."

"*Bien venue*, Mama." The threesome walked over to the long kitchen table where several conversations were going at once. As they placed the trays on the table, all conversations quieted. Alexandrine and Alice passed the cups to each person and offered banana bread to their guest first. Just then the younger ones, who had been playing in the yard or in the living room, burst into the room, eyes large as saucers.

"Can we have some too?" asked Henry and Edgar.

"Of course you may," answered Odile.

"*Merci*," said Poli as Alice handed him a plate.

"*Bien venue*, Poli," said Alice. As they lathered on the butter, conversations commenced. The men were discussing how early the snow would come this year based on the *Farmer's Almanac* and how severe a winter they could expect. Henry and Edgar giggled and made messes all over the floor.

"I just hope the snow waits until after Thanksgiving," continued Pierre. "There is still much to do before then."

"I personally would rather see snow than have freezing rain and sleet," said Odile. "It is so difficult to get around when everything is coated with ice."

"That may be, but you don't have to shovel rain and ice," said John, taking a piece of banana bread and stuffing half of it in his mouth.

"Spoken like a typical young man who doesn't wish to overdo it while the snow is coming down," said Pierre, as he slapped John on his back. This caused John to swallow some of the bread down the wrong pipe. He coughed and coughed until his face looked sunburned. As he finally settled down, he took a sip of coffee.

"I am sorry, John. I did not mean to make you choke," said Pierre.

"That's fine, Papa, I'll get you back someday when you least expect it." Everyone laughed and knew John meant every word. Pierre would need to watch his back in the future as his son was a true prankster.

"I am sure you will, son. Now shall we begin another game?"

"In a few minutes, Pierre," said Odile. "We are not all finished with our snack."

"Sorry, dear. I forget the ladies take small bites and twice as long to eat as the men." He winked.

"Oh, you," she said and threw a napkin at him. It hit him squarely on the forehead and he laughed uproariously. The afternoon continued in a merry way until it was time for the ladies to prepare supper.

Poli was invited to stay, but declined and headed back to the boardinghouse where Alice's grandmother was expecting him and the other boarders to have supper there. He thanked them all for the afternoon, tipped his hat, and strolled across the street. Alice glanced out the window and watched the six-foot frame saunter across the dirt road and take two steps at a time onto the porch and disappear through the front door. She turned and walked to the kitchen to help her mother and sister prepare meatloaf with mashed potatoes and green beans.

On Sunday morning, the family walked to Holy Family Church a few blocks away. The air was fresh and the sky a clear blue as they joined neighbors heading in the same direction. Sunday was a good day to catch up on the lives of their friends and neighbors and to go visiting family in the afternoon.

As they gathered into the narthex of the church and found an empty pew a few rows back from the front, Alice's thoughts wandered to the past weeks and prayed for direction. She asked the Lord if Poli would be part of her future. Although she didn't feel an instant peace about it, she knew she would have her answer when it was time for her to know.

The opening hymn, "Amazing Grace," was one of her favorites so she let her voice be heard and joined in the singing. Once the mass began and the scriptures were read, the pastor gave his homily. Today's message was about the prodigal son. Jesus told this parable about the father, who owned a lot of property and who had two sons and how one day the younger son asked for half of his inheritance. His father gave it to him, and a few days later the younger son left to a far country and used up all of his inheritance in a sinful manner.

Shortly after he had nothing left, a severe famine hit the land and he was reduced to caring for swine that ate better than he did. Starving and coming to his senses, he decided to return home and ask forgiveness of his father and to work as one of his slaves who were well fed. His father, searching for his son day after day, spotted him from a far distance and ran to him, hugging him and rejoicing that his son who was lost was now found.

The father held a huge party for him, which made the older son jealous because he toiled day after day and was never given anything to celebrate with his friends. He refused to join the crowd. His loving father told him gently that all that he owned was his, but they were celebrating because the son was "dead" and now was alive. The pastor made the analogy that God forgives our most grievous sins as long as we repent, because He is a loving God.

Alice took this message into account; however, she couldn't get out of her mind that Poli left home, perhaps not to squander away his father's possessions, but in an angry way. Would he decide to return to Canada and ask forgiveness and then remain there with his family? Would she lose him just as she was becoming rather fond of him? She barely concentrated on the rest of mass for her heart was in turmoil. She prayed for peace and that she would accept whatever God had in mind for her even if it meant her heart would be broken.

Chapter Twelve

WINTER IN MAINE

Winter arrived furiously as temperatures dropped into the teens. Snow swirled and the wind pushed all who dared venture into the elements. Visibility was a few inches in front of Alice's face as she trudged through knee-deep drifts on her way to the mills early one December morning. Her scarf, wrapped around her face with only her eyes peering over the top, helped her to breathe a little easier as the frosty wind whipped her coat and splattered her body with large snowflakes.

Bending forward and bracing herself against the force, her hands covered in mittens, she held on to her collar as she lifted her boots through the thick snow. Thankful for the pantaloons and other layers under her skirt, she plodded along, praying there would be heat in the mills when she arrived. The smokestacks a few hundred feet ahead blew gray clouds of smoke into the air, and the pungent scent made it to her nostrils. *Oh good, the heat must be on and I must be almost there,* she thought.

One reason Alice disliked working in the mills was that some of the women spoke vulgarities like the men. Her parents taught her to speak respectfully and not as though she was raised in a barn. Wishing there was other work she could do, she pondered what other jobs were available to a woman her age. Her thoughts turned to her suitor, and she wondered if her future held marriage to this man. Realizing she was falling in love with him made her blush despite the freezing temperatures.

Papa and Mama like Poli, so that's half the battle. Alexandrine, Alma, and John seem to enjoy his company too, and the little ones are always laughing at his antics. I think he'll fit well with our family. It's up to the good Lord to decide if he is the one for me, so I guess I will just keep on praying. With that thought in mind, she reached the entrance to the Goodall Mills and braced herself for another day of drudgery. She had made several nice friends there, which was a consolation.

At the end of her shift, Alice donned the many layers of clothing to brace herself against the storm that persistently held on throughout the day. Grateful she was on her way home, the walk became more bearable. She walked beside several friends until she reached Brook Street. There they continued on High Street and she marched up the hill and turned right onto Hammond Street, slipping and sliding on the road she was forced to walk in since the sidewalks were not clear.

Holding on to the railing of her home, Alice swiped her boot back and forth to clear the snow in her path as she ascended the front steps. As she entered the front door, she stomped her feet on the small rug to loosen some of the snow, hung her coat and scarf on a nearby hook, and pulled off her boots and placed them in the tray. Slipping into her shoes, she picked up her mittens and hat and headed to the kitchen where she would let them dry beside the woodstove.

"*Bonjour*, Mama, it smells good in here," said Alice. Little Yvonne crawled over to her as she warmed her hands by the stove. She lifted the child up high and she squealed.

"*Bonjour*, Alice. Be careful not to wiggle Yvonne too much; she just ate. How was your day at work? You must be frozen walking in this weather." Odile stirred a stew of hamburger, potatoes, and onions. Alice held on to the little girl, kissing her on the cheek.

"Work was more difficult today as many people did not make it in. The rest of us had to work extra hard keeping the machines going. I actually liked it inside today. It was warmer than being in that storm. I almost fell a few times coming back. It is very slippery out there."

Alice walked over to the crib in the living room to peek at the youngest addition to the family, Henedine, who was kicking her tiny legs and looking up at the ceiling. She gently touched her cheek and Henedine cooed. She left her playing with the edge of her blanket, placed Yvonne on the floor, and assisted her mother with preparing supper.

"Are you feeling all right, Mama? You look a little pale."

"Oh, I'm fine, just tired. I am not as young as I used to be, so bearing children at this age is more difficult. It sometimes feels a bit cramped in here, and I often wish we were on a farm with more space around us." She stirred the stew and placed the cover over it to simmer.

"You sit a while, Mama, as I finish up here," said Alice. "You need a rest."

Odile sat on one of the kitchen chairs and watched her daughter open a jar of pickled beets and pour some into a bowl. She moved quickly around the kitchen setting the table, taking out a loaf of bread, and chasing after Yvonne when she climbed where she wasn't supposed to climb. Odile knew it wouldn't be long before her daughter would be married, and she would miss her. The only consolation was that it would free up some space in her home for her large family. Eight children aged twenty down to infancy were exhausting even though she was only thirty-six years old.

Once Alice had completed the preparations, she fed the youngest children. Her other siblings and father arrived a short time later, and they gathered together for the evening meal.

"Mama, this sure is good, especially on such a cold day as this," said Alexandrine.

"*Merci*, Alexandrine. How was work for you today?"

"Same as always, but at least it was warm inside. The wind is so strong it nearly pushed me down. Oh, I almost forgot. I heard today that Monsieur Gagne has passed away. He had been sick for several days and last night he died."

Odile wiped her mouth with her cloth napkin and laid it on her lap. She looked up at Alexandrine and said, "I am sorry to hear that. I had not heard he was sick. How old was he, and how is Madame Gagne?"

"Celeste, you remember her, my friend from shop? Well she said that he was eighty-four years old. Madame Gagne is doing the best she can. Her children are nearby so they are there to help her." She scooped some stew into her spoon and took a bite.

"I will make extra for supper tomorrow night if you don't mind bringing it to her."

"I can do that, Mama. She is just on North Avenue. Hopefully it won't be snowing tomorrow."

"I will wrap the plate up good so it will stay warm until you get there."

"Good."

A couple of days later, some of the family attended the funeral for Mr. Gagne and expressed their sympathies to his widow and his family. He would be buried in the spring, but in the meantime his body would be in the vault at the cemetery until the ground thawed.

Odile's family checked in on Mrs. Gagne several times over the weeks, sometimes helping with shoveling snow, bringing a meal over, or shopping for a few necessities when her adult children were not able. She was very grateful and shared homemade cookies with the children when they stopped in.

The neighborhood markets were within walking distance to their home, which made it easier to get by without depending on others while Pierre was at work. Odile made a list and sent her teenaged children to get the necessary grocery items, which they carried back in their arms, slipping and sliding on the streets. Milk and cream were delivered to their home by an area dairy farmer and kept in an icebox.

Alice continued seeing Poli as he visited and played cards with the family on the weekends. The snow continued to pile up, and the oxen used to clear the snow or pull a roller over the streets were kept in shape by the road commissioner.

*　*　*

As spring neared, Odile had a feeling Alice would soon be engaged and she would be planning a wedding. Alice's eyes lit up every time the name *Poli* was mentioned. In June she would be twenty-one years old. *To think I was a widow with four children at age twenty-one,* she thought. *It feels like a whole lifetime ago. Where have the years gone? Here I am no longer thin, with a nearly twenty-one-year-old daughter and the possibility of a son-in-law, then maybe grandchildren, when my youngest are still in diapers. Come to think of it, my mother still had little ones when I was married at fifteen. That was different. Papa arranged my marriage back then. Alice has a choice, and it is good she has waited. Oh well, time will tell how things turn out.*

Odile busied herself with sewing and mending clothes, washing laundry, cleaning up after four young children, and cooking and baking.

Adversity helps make someone strong physically and emotionally. She realized she was no longer the meek young girl of fifteen, but she had become a rather strong-willed woman who could hold her own. She had learned much from her children's schoolbooks as well as listening to adults around her.

Months of colds and influenza finally passed, and spring awakened with tiny purple crocuses peeking through dead leaves and showing off their beauty. The air, freshened from early spring rains, gave new life to the grass, flower beds, trees, and to people, lightening their moods. On one delightful sunny day, Odile heard a knock and as she approached the door, she recognized the familiar stance of a tall young man. She wiped her hands on her apron and turned the knob.

"Well, *bonjour*, Poli, come on in," she said as she opened the door wider. "Alice is not home right now."

Poli stood holding his hat, turning the edges nervously.

"What's wrong, Poli?"

"Umm, nothing, nothing is wrong. I, uh, wondered if I could speak with Monsieur Laprise. Is he home?" Odile understood why he had come.

Chapter Thirteen

ALICE'S WEDDING DAY

Quiet, rapid footsteps caused the floorboards to squeak as Alice paced from one end of her bedroom to the other, nervously getting ready. Odile smiled as she prepared breakfast in her kitchen below and reminisced about days past. Her firstborn was now a lovely, slim, healthy young woman, while her own body had expanded several sizes from giving birth to eight children.

Odile shrugged and turned her attention back to the day. Stirrings of others in the household blended in while her hand stirred the muffin batter. She poured it into prepared tins. Bacon was frying in the pan on the woodstove as she slipped the muffin pans into the warm oven.

Her mind wandered once again to the day Alice was born and all that had happened in those few years following. Odile could not believe the time had flown so quickly. Some days it felt like a blink of an eye, and others it felt as though she had lived a few different lives. Soon the family would be gathered for their last meal in the fashion they have been accustomed to. Alice would be married and starting her own traditions. Odile sighed. *Oh, how I will miss my girl.*

A few hours later, organ music played as Pierre Laprise held Alice's arm as they slowly strode up the center aisle of Holy Family Church while wide-eyed children, family, and friends lined pews on both sides. Alice quivered although it was a hot, humid August morning. Her veil and wedding dress were borrowed from her mother's first wedding. Alice smiled nervously as she neared Napoleon. Her mother stood at the first pew on the right, beaming and crying at the same time. Pierre lifted his daughter's veil, kissed her on the cheek, and guided her to Napoleon who gently held her hand, and together they turned and faced the priest. Pierre took his place beside his wife and younger children.

Reverend McGinnis performed the Catholic wedding mass on August 16, 1920, at Holy Family Church on North Avenue, Sanford. Promising to love, honor, and be faithful to each other until death, Napoleon and Alice stood holding hands near the altar. Prayers and music filled the air with happiness and joy as two became one in the eyes of the Lord. Symbolic rings were exchanged as a reminder that the circle is never to be broken except by death. The traditional mass was celebrated with the culmination of Communion and a final blessing.

Reverend McGinnis said, "I now pronounce you man and wife. You may kiss your bride." Poli gave his new bride a quick kiss on the lips, and Alice blushed.

As the young couple turned to face those congregated in their presence, Reverend McGinnis said to the crowd, "I wish to introduce to you, Mr. and Mrs. Napoleon Alexandre." Cheers and clapping resounded off the paneled walls as the organ played the wedding march.

Following the mass, family and friends met at Hammond Street for the reception. Much fun and laughter was heard throughout the neighborhood as the newlywed couple made their rounds, talking with all who celebrated their special day with them. Congratulations and words of advice were given before the couple departed for Old Orchard Beach for their honeymoon.

At the end of the day, Odile dropped into a chair and rubbed her swollen, hot feet. Mixed feelings of joy and sadness enveloped her as her eldest daughter began her new life as Mrs. Napoleon J. Alexandre—joy that Alice was happy and sadness that her eldest moved out of the nest. She remembered her own wedding day at age fifteen and how she had been so frightened and unhappy.

Her thoughts went way back to that day when she walked up the aisle with her father: *Oh, Lord, please let me wake up from this nightmare. This cannot be happening to me. Octave is old enough to be my own father.* Her grip on her father's arm had tightened and her legs trembled as they continued the slow walk toward the altar. She had tried to smile, but was afraid she'd burst out crying, so she stared straight ahead as her father held on. Her thoughts had raced at that point: *Papa must think if he lets go I will turn around and run out the back door. I can barely breathe. How will I get through this day and pretend to be happy like most brides I've watched? Oh, God, give me strength especially tonight when we're alone and he'll expect me to—*

"Mama, Mama." Odile heard Yvonne beside her as she broke into her thoughts. The little girl had tears running down her cheeks as Odile placed her on her lap.

"What's the matter, Yvonne? Are you hurt?" Odile did a quick check of her child.

"No, Mama." She sniffed. "Alice is gone. I miss her."

Odile hugged her child, comforting her. "Sshhhh, it'll be all right. Alice will visit often. She's going to live just around the corner. You'll see. She'll be coming by to see us." The sobs quieted, and Yvonne wiggled herself off her mother's lap and ran to her papa as he entered the kitchen, holding Henedine.

When the married couple returned from their honeymoon in Salem, MA, they made their home in a rented apartment on Sherburne Street, a short walk away from Alice's family. They continued working as mill hands at Goodall Mills. Alice visited her parents and younger siblings as often as she could. Yvonne often greeted her at the door and gave her a big hug. Alice pondered when she would begin a family of her own.

Chapter Fourteen

HER FIRSTBORN

While still living on Sherburne Street, Alice gave birth to their firstborn, Joseph Arthur, on August 28, 1921, one year after their wedding. Alice stopped working at the mills and Poli searched for some property to buy. Joseph was a tiny baby with a narrow face and ears that bent forward, and he was well loved by his parents, grandparents, aunts, and uncles.

Odile visited often to see her first grandchild even though some of her children were still young and she was expecting her ninth child and feeling worn out. The humidity was stifling as she wiped her face with her embroidered handkerchief. Multiple times a day she fanned herself with anything she could find—an envelope, a notebook, a magazine, anything to bring relief.

"Oh, how I love little babies," Odile said during one visit to her daughter and grandson. She held him tight against her and rocked him gently as she hummed a song. Baby Joseph cooed sweetly in her plump embrace.

"I remember the day you were born, Alice. I was in labor a long time, but when I finally delivered you, thoughts of the pain went away as I looked at your tiny fingers and toes and your sweet little face. It does not seem possible that many years have gone by and now you have your own little one to love."

Alice pulled up a chair beside her mother and said, "I'm sorry it took me so long to come, Mama. Was I a good baby or did I cry a lot and keep you up all night?"

"You only fussed when you were hungry, and of course every baby wakes up several times a night to be fed. Yes, I'd say you were a good baby. As long as I changed your diaper often, you were content."

Mother and daughter looked lovingly at the little bundle nestled in his cotton blanket. "Soon he won't need that blanket today, it is going to be another hot one," said Alice. "I like the cool evenings, though; it makes it easier to sleep."

"August does have those nice cool evenings and warm days. It stays warmer longer here than in Canada. You probably don't remember that as you were just a child when we moved here."

"Do you miss Canada, Mama?" Alice asked.

"Oh, *oui*, I do miss it very much, especially the rest of the family, my friends, and the farm. Here, we are all too close together. No room for much of a garden or a place for the children to play. They end up in the street or down at the park." Odile closed her eyes and conjured up the faces and places she'd left behind, and she sighed. "I guess we will never go back. I never thought I would have to leave like I had seen others do over the years. It is truly sad."

Alice laid her hand on her mother's shoulder as tears formed in her eyes. She also remembered the day they arrived in Sanford, Maine, when she was a little girl and how afraid and confused she was with people talking in a strange language. She wondered if she would have met Poli if they had stayed in Canada. They lived in the same village but her family did not know his family. She shrugged and thought, *I guess it was meant to be to come to this strange land and meet Poli, and for that I am grateful.*

"Well, I think it's time to get dinner ready," said Alice. "Will you be staying, Mama?"

"No, no. I should get back home and fix something for your papa and the children. Thank you anyway." Odile pushed herself up and walked Joseph to his tiny crib and laid him down on his side propping a pillow behind him. She straightened her dress around her bulging belly and gave Alice's hand a squeeze.

"Make sure you take a nap this afternoon while Joseph takes his nap. I will talk with you later on."

"I will try to nap, Mama, but I don't usually have the time nor do I get sleepy. While he is sleeping I get caught up on my sewing and housework." She smiled and watched her mother gather her young children who were on the porch, cross the street, waddle to the corner, and turn toward Hammond Street.

Alice tied an apron around her waist and prepared dinner for herself and Poli because he would be coming home today during his break and would be very hungry. She wished he could find work he really enjoyed doing. Being a mill hand was not his cup of tea, and he preferred working outside on a farm or in the woods.

Poli arrived shortly after noon, hungry as a bear out of hibernation. He washed up at the kitchen sink and gave his bride a kiss and a hug. "How has your day been so far?" he asked.

"Just fine. Mama came by for a visit. She loves little babies." She smiled as she watched her husband walk over to the crib. She whispered, "How is your day? Is it very hot in the mill today?"

Poli walked back and sat down at the head of the table. "*Oui*, it is getting hot in there today. It was cool first thing this morning, but with the temperature rising outside, it is warming up quickly inside. This looks good, Alice."

Alice sat down kitty-corner to him and bowed her head as they said grace.

When finished with the prayer, she said, "I do not miss that at all. I was thinking this morning that I hope you find a job you like doing. It makes for a long day doing something you don't enjoy." They ate quietly for a few moments.

Poli spoke, "I have been asking around town if anyone knows of work on a farm or logging trees. Maybe something will come up soon."

"I have been saving as much as I can from your pay so we can find our own piece of land to build a house. Then we can start our own farm. What do you think?" said Alice.

"Good. I think that's good. Let's go over the numbers tonight. I know you are really smart with figuring. Do you think you could teach me how to read and write? I did not get very far in school, as you know, because of the farm back home, but I think it would be good for me to learn. I know a little, but not much, and it's embarrassing. Maybe I will own my own business someday, and I would need to be able to read the paperwork."

Alice finished chewing and said, "I was hoping you would ask sometime. I would be happy to teach you what I know."

Poli winked at his wife and finished his dinner. The baby stirred and awoke, so Poli pushed his chair back and sauntered to the crib. He picked up the infant in his large hands and said, "*Bonjour, petit garcon.* Are you hungry? Or did we wake you up from all our talking?" Turning to Alice, he said, "Look who's awake, Mama."

Alice stood and smiled. Touching the small red face, she said, "Looks like Papa and Mama woke you up, little one." As he snuggled in his father's arms, Alice cleaned up the table and put the dirty dishes in the sink. She knew Joseph would start crying soon to be fed; however, right now he was content to be cradled in his father's arms, staring up into his face.

After Poli left for work, Alice fed her son and put him down for his afternoon nap. She mended clothes, washed and dried the dishes, and prepared the vegetables for the supper meal. She rested about ten minutes—just enough to rejuvenate her body for the rest of the day.

A couple of weeks after Joseph was born, Alice's sister, Alexandrine, ran over with the smaller siblings in tow to tell her that their mother was in labor. The midwife had arrived and shooed them out of their home. Hours went by and Alexandrine went over to see if there was any news yet. She returned a half hour later, winded from running, to tell Alice and the others that their mother just gave birth to a baby girl.

"Mama named her Annette. I only saw her for a second. She is all wrinkly, but she's cute. Mama is very tired, so I need to go back there and help Madame Sylvestre. Would you mind keeping the others for a while until they tell me it's time to bring them home?"

"*Oui*, of course, they can stay. John and Alma can help me with the younger ones. Tell Mama I'll be praying for her and the baby. Go on now and help out." Alexandrine started for the door, and Alice called out to her, "Alexandrine, don't worry. Everything will be fine with Mama and with us here. Let them stay for supper and come back for them after six o'clock or so."

"*Merci*, Alice," she responded and closed the screen door. Alice watched as her sister ran down the street and turned the corner, her long braided hair bouncing off her back.

Pauvre, Mama. She must be so tired and I'm not there to help. My little baby is already an uncle! Alice thought to herself. She turned her attention to her siblings and decided they should spend some time outside on this beautiful September day before tackling their homework.

Chapter Fifteen

ODILE VISITS: 1927

At nearly six years old, Joseph helped his mama with a few household chores before heading outside to play. He disliked some of those household chores, but he was expected to help since he was now the big brother to Raymond, George, and Adrienne.

Being a small child, he found it difficult to handle a broom. Floors needed to be swept daily due to the dirt driveway, especially as the dirt jammed into the soles of shoes on rainy days. Joseph made his small piles and then held the dust pan as his mother swept the dirt into it. Then he'd pick up the dust pan and dump the dirt back outside. His grandmother, Odile, had nicknamed him "Petit Pete" because of his small stature, so now almost everyone in his family called him Pete. Most neighbors and friends, however, still called him Joseph. Joseph also piled wood with his mama and stacked it neatly in rows in the shed attached to the rear of the house.

Napoleon had bought a parcel of land on High Street and moved a nearby building, nicknamed "the potato house" because it's where they used to house potatoes, onto the lot. He added a second floor to make additional bedrooms for his growing family. They had chickens and cows, and Poli talked about getting a pig and a horse.

Mama and Joseph planted a vegetable garden in the full sun on the easterly side of the green clapboard house. Poli and his neighbors had worked diligently to clear the area of trees and stumps. Tomatoes, green peppers, string beans, potatoes, corn, peas, carrots, turnips, cabbage, onions, radishes, and cucumbers had been planted in the soft brown earth at the end of May after the last frost. Keeping up with the weeds without pulling out the new shoots was a difficult task for a young boy so Alice took the job upon herself. Kneeling on the ground, she bent to pluck the small weeds before they became troublesome. Pausing periodically to wipe the sweat from her brow with her apron, she stretched her sore back and felt the sun on her face. She moved sideways along each row until the job was complete.

On most weekends Alice's parents came by for a visit with their youngest children in tow. The children played with their niece and nephews as they were so close in age. They visited often, walking approximately one mile each way. Pierre was now working as a traveling furniture salesman and sometimes worked on Saturdays. Annette was their last child and was close to six years old, like Joseph. Alice's brother John had his own place now, and Alexandrine and Alma were also adults and busy with their own lives.

One day when Odile was visiting and the children were outside playing, she said to her eldest daughter as she plopped herself into a kitchen chair, "I sure am glad I am no longer bearing children. I think nine is enough. I am worn out."

Alice chuckled as she placed a piece of raisin pie on a plate and offered it to her mother. "I know how you feel, Mama," she said as she rubbed her round tummy. "With the four plus Adrien, God rest his soul, and this little one who will be here next month, I have often wondered how you managed having four young ones, becoming a widow, moving hundreds of miles from your homeland, and later starting another family and having five more children. You must have the strength of an ox."

Odile laughed and said, "Oh no, if I were as strong as an ox, I would not be so tired. Just remember to pray each day for strength from the *bon Dieux*, and He will help you through it all. Humans can't do it all alone." She took a bite from the warm raisin pie as they continued talking and filling each other in with the latest in family news. Alice's great-grandparents still had boarders to supplement Pepere's income.

"Thank you, Mama, for teaching me so much about cooking and taking care of a home. I would be lost if I hadn't learned how to start a fire in the woodstove, cook meals, sew clothes, plant a garden, and so many other things. I do not, however, wish to milk a cow. I am happy that Poli and Petit Pete are taking care of that chore. It is so gross."

Odile laughed heartily and said, "I remember milking many cows when we lived in Canada, and I can't say it was my favorite thing to do either. Although after your father died in that winter storm, I found myself having no choice on some days when the neighbors were unable to get to us because the weather was too blustery. The cows would have been in too much pain otherwise. I would draw up my skirts through the deep snow to the barn and take care of them. We tied a rope from the porch to the barn to direct our path on blustery days because we couldn't see a thing. Sometimes we have to do things that are very unpleasant to survive. Mmmm, this pie is good."

Alice leaned back against her chair after finishing her pie and laid her hands on her large tummy. Her short, dark hair was pulled back with bobby pins and her dark eyes nearly closed when she smiled. She heard the squeals of the children in the backyard and wondered if her next child would be a girl or another boy and what name she would give him or her.

"I think this little one is another boy," Alice said to Odile. "I am carrying him the same way I carried all the boys, and he is rather rambunctious in there." Alice felt good discussing her pregnancy with her mother because that was not something that could be discussed with children present. The children thought the Indians dropped off the babies, and she would rather let them believe that than be embarrassed in explaining otherwise.

Her mother interrupted her thoughts by answering, "I hope we will be able to get some of your canning done before *he* decides to make his appearance. July can be such a hot month, and I always found it more difficult to carry during the summer. At least when you were born it was June and we were not yet in the hottest part of the summer heat." She paused. "Sometimes it feels like yesterday and other times like it was a lifetime ago." The two sat in silence with their own thoughts for a few moments before a child slammed the back door and ran crying toward the women.

"Annette, what is the matter? Are you hurt somewhere?" Odile gently lifted her daughter onto her plump lap. The little girl hiccupped repeatedly against her mother's chest as she rocked her back and forth.

After a few minutes the sniffling subsided and her sad red eyes looked up as she spoke. "Mama, the boys won't let me play hide-go-seek with them, and they pushed me away." She sniffled and Odile wiped her daughter's nose with her handkerchief.

"Well, now, my little one, I will go speak with them. You stay with Alice and I will be right back." Odile stood and placed the little girl on the chair, smoothing out her damp hair, and walked to the back door. The screen door opened and gently closed behind her as she stepped into the backyard. Placing her hand above her brow to block the sun, she scanned the yard for the little rascals. She spotted her eldest grandson counting against the barn and strode over to him before he reached number twenty.

"Petit Pete, I need to speak with you, please." He jumped and turned when he heard his grandmother's voice, not expecting anyone to come up behind him.

"What do you want, Memere?" asked the little boy.

"Annette came in the house crying. She said you boys wouldn't let her play with you, and I want to know why," she stated gently.

Joseph looked around for reinforcements, but all the children were hiding, so he was on his own. He looked down at his feet, shuffling back and forth, and finally said, "Well, I don't know."

"I think you do know. You just don't want to tell me, is that it?" She lowered herself so she could face him at his level. "Would you please tell me the truth?"

"She always wants to hide with one of us instead of finding her own place. So we told her to go away. She's such a baby sometimes." He blurted it out before he realized to whom he was speaking. He quickly covered his mouth as if to take the words back and his wide eyes stared up at his grandmother.

Odile thought for a minute and looked at her frightened little grandson. The other children remained out of sight as she searched the yard with her eyes. She stood back up and looked at Joseph and said, "Sometimes children want to hide with others because they think it's more fun, and sometimes they are a little bit scared and don't want to be forgotten. I would like you and the other children to talk about what you have done to Annette and then come in and say you're sorry. I will talk with her about what you said and maybe we can work something out together."

"All right, Memere." He let out a long breath.

"Now, one more thing. Think about how you would feel if someone treated you like you just treated Annette. Would you think it was fair? Don't answer right now, but think about it." Odile bent to hug her eldest grandchild and walked back toward the house. She heard him say, "Ready or not here I come," before he dashed around the barn. She knew after all the children were done getting caught, they would whisper together and come into the house and apologize.

A short while later Annette was outside laughing and playing with her siblings and her niece and nephews, and all was well once again. Alice and Odile continued their conversation until it was time for Odile and her children to walk the mile or so back home.

Odile Jalbert

Octave Morneau

Alice (Morneau) and Napoleon Alexandre's Wedding, Aug. 1920

Back: Napoleon and Alice
Front: Raymond, George and Joseph

Alice Alexandre with twins, Adrien and Adrienne

Joseph "Pete", Adrienne, Raymond, George and Edgar (front)

Edgar, Roland and Adrienne

Napoleon with 2-horned moose and cow, High Pine, Wells, 1932

High Street home

Joseph "Pete", George and Raymond

Joseph "Pete" Alexandre on Blackie (LaNoir) by wood pile

Pierre and Odile (Morneau) Laprise

Back row left to right: Juliette, Joseph, George, Raymond,
Roland, Henri, Adrienne, Henriette, and Anita
Second row L-R: Ronald, Roger, Alice (Morneau) Alexandre,
Shirley, Napoleon Alexandre, Louis and Andre
Front row: Therese (standing), and Gerard (sitting)

Chapter Sixteen

EDGAR IS BORN: 1927

July 17, 1927, began with a lovely easterly breeze blowing through the open windows on High Street. The children awoke to the sound of an infant crying and rushed into the kitchen to see their father speaking with Madame L'Heureux. He turned his attention to his children and bent down on one knee and said, "Come here, *mez enfants*, I have something to tell you." The children gathered around their father with sleepy eyes and disheveled hair. "A new baby came during the night."

"Is that who's crying, Papa?" asked Raymond.

"*Oui*, that's him all right."

"It's a boy? Where did he come from? Is he our brother?" asked three-year-old George.

"Just hold on, not so fast," said Papa, chuckling. "Yes, he is a boy and he is your brother. You will get to meet him soon. He needs to be fed right now." Poli decided not to answer the second question and hoped his young son forgot about it. He raised himself to his full height, and the children leaned their heads back so as to see his face.

"I'm hungry. Where's Mama?" asked Joseph.

"She's in the bedroom feeding the baby. Madame L'Heureux is going to help get some breakfast for you. Sit down at the table and she'll be ready in a little while. I need to go out to the barn. I'll be back soon." Poli rubbed his large palms on their heads, creating a bigger mess with their hair, and left through the back door.

"Good morning children, how are you doing today?" asked Madame L'Heureux as she entered the kitchen.

"Good," they said in unison.

"What's for breakfast, Madame L'Heureux?" asked Raymond.

"I am cooking your mama's crepes with some bacon on the side."

"Mmmm, that's my favorite." Raymond rubbed his little tummy and licked his lips, and the other children laughed.

Fifteen-month-old Adrienne stirred in her crib, and Madame L'Heureux went to check on her after putting crepes and bacon on each of the children's plates. After changing the toddler's wet diaper, she carried her into the kitchen and placed her in her high chair. Using an old belt, she tied her in securely and placed a bib around her neck. Adrienne banged on her tray and giggled at her siblings, and the children laughed. Madame L'Heureux cut up a crepe into tiny pieces and placed it on Adrienne's tray. Soon Adrienne was stuffing them into her mouth with her tiny hands.

"Madame L'Heureux, can I have another crepe please?" asked Joseph.

"Me, too, please?" asked Raymond.

"Sure, I will cook one up for each of you. Where did you put them all? In your toes?"

The boys giggled and nearly fell off their chairs. A few minutes later each of the two eldest boys had a hot crepe on his plate. Madame L'Heureux left to check on Alice and the baby, returning a few minutes later.

"Your baby brother is asleep and your mama is resting. Try to be a little quieter if you can please."

"*Oui*, Madame L'Heureux, we will try," said Joseph.

"What's the baby's name?" asked Raymond.

"Well, I don't know. I will ask your papa or your mama in a little while."

Poli came in the back door and gently closed the door behind him. He hung his hat on the hook by the door and sauntered into the kitchen. After washing his hands at the kitchen sink, he sat at the table and Madame L'Heureux handed him a cup of coffee.

"*Merci*, Madame L'Heureux," he said.

"*Bien venue*," she replied.

"Papa, what's the name of our baby brother?" asked Raymond in between a mouthful of bacon.

"Mama and I decided on Edgar. What do you think of that?"

"Good, Papa. Is he big or small?"

Poli took a sip of coffee and responded, "Well, all babies are small, but I would say he is bigger than the other babies we've had so far."

"Really, really big… like a hundred pounds?" Joseph's eyes widened with excitement.

Poli nearly spit out his coffee and roared with laughter. The tiny infant in the next room awoke, letting his dad and siblings know he was not happy.

"Oh, oh, I think I woke up baby Edgar," said Poli as he covered his mouth with his palm and cleaned the mess he'd made. "Mama will not be happy with me either," he whispered. He glanced over his shoulder to see Madame L'Heureux walk into the bedroom, closing the door behind her. Soon the baby was consoled and quieted down. Some of the older children covered their mouths, too, as their shoulders shook with mirth.

"Papa, how much does he weigh?"

"Oh, I would say maybe seven pounds or so."

"Well, that's not very much. I thought you said he was bigger than the other babies. You're teasing me, Papa," said little Joseph, disappointed that his brother wasn't huge.

Papa placed his hand on his son's shoulder and said, "Don't you remember when Adrienne was born? She only weighed about four pounds and little Adrien too. How much do you weigh do you think?"

Joseph shrugged his small shoulders.

"I think you weigh between thirty and forty pounds, so if Edgar weighed a hundred, he'd be bigger than you. What would you think of that?"

His son pondered this for a moment, his mouth twitching back and forth. Finally he responded, "I don't think that would be very fair.

Mama wouldn't be able to carry him either. Would he be as big as you, Papa?"

Poli smiled with that twinkle in his eye and said, "No he wouldn't be quite as big as me, *mon petit garcon*, but he'd be getting pretty close." Poli continued to sip his coffee when Madame L'Heureux returned to the kitchen.

With one hand on her hip, she looked at Poli and chided, "The baby is back to sleep now, but Alice is awake. You need to be a little quieter as I asked the children to be before you came in." She shook her finger at him playfully and began cleaning up after the children. Poli smirked at his children and they started giggling. Madame L'Heureux looked over at him and shook her head. "You're as bad as the children," she said, "if not worse."

Poli finished his coffee and stood as he responded to her, "That may be true, but my wife loves me that way." He grinned and headed toward the bedroom, his children giggling at the table.

"Now, children, since you're done with your breakfast, go wash up and play outside for a while so Mama and baby can sleep. Please stay away from your mama's flowers."

"*Oui*, Madame L'Heureux," they said as they pushed away from the table.

Madame L'Heureux cleaned up Adrienne and placed her on the floor once the older children had gone outside. She then proceeded to clean the dishes and the table. A few minutes later, Poli entered the kitchen and informed her that Alice and Edgar were resting and he'd be out in the barn if she needed him, and later he would fetch the doctor to check on Alice and the baby.

As was usual, Alice didn't need much rest to feel revived, so she lay quietly praying that her newborn baby and her other children would be healthy and safe. She prayed also that the good Lord would see fit to provide for their needs, enough food for their bellies and enough money to pay for material to make clothes for her growing family and to maintain their home. Alice prayed daily for her family and for strength to handle whatever she needed to accomplish and whatever catastrophe might happen during the day. Her Joseph was always getting scrapes more than the other children. She just prayed that nothing worse would happen.

Chapter Seventeen

CANNING

Hot blistery temperatures and thunderstorms filled the next few days as northeasterly breezes filtered in through the windows. Alice was grateful for the breezes, especially when the woodstove was heated up to cook meals. The garden was flourishing well and the fresh vegetables added much flavor to their daily meals. On sweltering days, the meals consisted of corn on the cob, sliced cucumbers, tomatoes, and radishes, with bread on the side.

A few weeks later, Alice and Odile prepared to can the garden vegetables. Together they retrieved canning jars from the basement and washed and inspected them to make sure there were no cracks or chips. They counted to make sure they had enough rubber seals to secure each jar, plus enough salt, vinegar, and spices. The large canning pot was filled with water and placed on a burner on the woodstove. The first day they canned eighteen quarts of green beans, sealing them with red rubber seals and snapping the clamps down on the glass lids before boiling them in a hot water bath for twenty minutes.

On the second day they canned dill pickles, and on the third day they canned carrots. In August the tomatoes were ready for canning, filling thirty-one quarts. As August wound down, the green tomatoes, green peppers, and onions were used to make piccalilli and stored in pint jars. All the jars were carried into the basement and stored on shelves. Odile took some home to her family as well for their winter survival.

On the last day of canning, the ladies sat at the kitchen table, wiping their brows with hand-crocheted handkerchiefs, their aprons dirty from their difficult task. Alice said to her mother, "I sure am glad that's all done. I cannot believe it's almost September."

"Yes, me too. It's hot work having the stove going and lifting heavy pots of water and pulling the rack out with seven full jars of hot vegetables. My arms ache today."

"My back aches and my feet are sore. Thank the Lord. Edgar has been a good baby through all of this. He's little enough to still need lots of sleep. Adrienne is walking all over the place now, so I have to keep a close eye on her when she's in the kitchen. At least when the weather is nice, the older children watch her outside."

"I can't believe Little Pete is now six, and my Annette will also be six in a few days and going to school."

"*Oui*, school starts soon, and Joseph is not looking forward to it. He enjoys being outside and does not want to be cooped up in school all day. He'd rather be in the woods playing or around the farm animals, just like his papa."

"He will get used to it just like we all did," said Odile. "I suppose it is harder for some children to adjust than for others. At least in first grade they do some fun things in class, not just math and reading. Who knows, maybe he will enjoy it."

"I certainly hope so, Mama. I am all of a sudden very hungry. Would you care for a piece of blueberry pie and a cup of coffee or tea?" asked Alice.

"*Oui*, pie and tea sounds good to me. Is it still your favorite?"

Alice placed her dark hair behind her ear as she sliced the pie and said, "Oh *oui*, it is still my favorite. I never tire of eating blueberry pie. However, cleaning all those tiny wild blueberries takes a long time and, in this house, the pies do not last long." She winked at her dear mother as she handed her a plate with blueberries oozing out of the crust. "I also still love salmon pie. It's especially good on cold winter days."

The teakettle whistled and Alice pulled down two teacups and saucers from the shelf and set them on the table. She retrieved the teakettle and poured hot water into each cup. Pulling two spoons from her front apron pocket, she handed one to her mother and stirred her cup with the other.

"I remember when almost all the children lived under the same roof and how quickly the pies and cookies disappeared. I always wished it would be as easy to make them as to eat them." Odile chuckled and scooped up a bite of pie.

Just then Joseph, Raymond, George, and Adrienne rushed in the back door and, noticing the pie on the table, asked if they could each have a piece. Alice and Odile shared a laugh as the children washed their hands and hungrily stared at the pie. Alice ate her last bite and stood to wait on her youngsters.

"No rest for the weary," she said to her mother who winked at her. After placing a plate with a slice of pie in front of each of her children, Alice heard a sound from the bedroom and said, "Oh, I hear Edgar. I will be back shortly."

Odile smiled and watched her growing brood of grandchildren as blue tongues licked the outer edges of their mouths. She spoon-fed Adrienne as the little girl tried persistently to grab the spoon from her *memere*. Twenty minutes later Alice returned with Edgar, who had been fed and had on a fresh cloth diaper pinned with large safety pins.

"He's as happy as a clam now," said Alice as she cradled Edgar gently in her arms. "He was a very hungry boy and had a very wet diaper. Didn't you, little one?" She directed the last sentence to her infant son.

"He sure is growing fast. May I hold him a bit before we head home?" asked Odile.

"Of course, here you go. He feels as though he has gained at least five pounds in only a month and a half."

Odile smiled at her sixth grandchild, ran her index finger along his cheek and chin, and gave him a peck on the forehead. She continued speaking to him in her grandmotherly fashion as the older children hovered around them. They smoothed the top of his head and played with his tiny fingers like gentle lambs.

Alice looked at her family with the blue lips and said, "Time for you, children, to go clean your teeth. Remember to use the baking soda and scrub well."

"Oh, Mama, can't we play with the baby a little while longer? Please?" George asked.

"You may play with him after you clean up. Now go on all of you. Scoot."

The children dashed toward the washroom and quickly cleaned their blue teeth and returned to the kitchen in record time. A short while later, Odile and her children left and Alice's eldest ran back outside to play for the remainder of the afternoon.

Around supper time, Joseph helped his father in the barn as it was time to milk the cows. Raymond and George set the table. A couple of hours after supper, Alice tucked them all into bed and pondered what was in store for them tomorrow.

Chapter Eighteen

SCHOOL DAYS

School began on a Wednesday after Labor Day, the first day for Joseph and his little aunt, Annette. Poli walked his young son to the corner of Grammar Street where Mr. Shaw would pick up some of the schoolchildren with his horse and buggy and take them to the new Edison School on Lebanon Street. Before school started, Poli had taken Joseph to the school to meet his teacher. Poli told him that he would meet new friends and would be able to walk to Grammar Street with these children.

"Papa, I don't want to go to school. Can I stay home please?" Joseph muttered.

Poli lowered himself down to eye level with Joseph and said, "Joseph, it is important to go to school so you can learn to write words and read and know how to count numbers. This will help you when you get older. Do you understand?"

"No I don't. Why do I have to go in that big building instead of staying home and playing? It's not fair that Raymond, George, and Adrienne don't have to go."

"Raymond will have his turn next year, and then George the next year after that, and so on. They have to be six years old first before going to school. Since you are six already, it is time for you to go. You will like it, you'll see. Just give it a try, okay?"

Joseph lowered his head and said, "Okay, Papa. I'll try."

"That's my boy. Mr. Shaw is coming."

On his way home, Poli recalled their visit to the school the day before. The two had walked up the front steps of the red brick building on the corner of Lebanon and Oxford Streets. Poli introduced himself to the teacher and she welcomed Joseph to first grade. Joseph looked at the floor when his teacher asked him if he was anxious to start school. Poli nudged him to respond, and Joseph shook his head. His teacher explained what they would be learning and how much fun they would have, but Poli could tell Joseph didn't look very interested.

When they left the classroom, Poli asked Joseph why he wouldn't speak to his teacher, and Joseph shrugged his shoulders and said he didn't want to go to school; he wanted to stay home and play outside. Poli explained that he would get used to it if he gave it a chance and he might even learn to like it. Arriving at home, Poli told Alice what had transpired, and she sent a prayer to heaven to keep her son in His care.

At noon the children were dismissed to their homes for dinner, and those who lived close enough walked back and forth to school. Joseph was too far so he remained at the school until Mr. Shaw returned to gather up the children for the ride back to High Street.

Joseph returned home with Poli that afternoon full of information about his day and the names of new friends he'd made. Arrangements were made with neighboring parents that their children would walk together to Grammar Street. Little by little, Joseph became more accustomed to school and the regiment of classroom time, yet he still preferred the great outdoors. His teacher kept the children occupied with different subjects to keep their attention span in check.

As soon as the bell rang at the end of the school day, Joseph and his friends dashed through the front doors, anxious to get home to play hide-and-seek or baseball.

As winter approached, cardboard boxes were dismantled in order to lay flat to get ready for sledding and then stored in the barn until the snow arrived. Alice prepared stews and chowders and bought fresh loaves of bread to keep her family warm and nurtured. In the evenings she spent time mending clothing and sewing new clothes. She knitted mittens and crocheted handkerchiefs, rocking gently in her rocking chair. On cold winter nights, she slept in her rocker to periodically stoke the fire and add wood so that their home would stay reasonably warm, at least on the first floor.

The farm provided for their needs, and Poli logged wood to sell from a lot he had purchased. Piles of wood lay stacked on the edge of the driveway as Poli used a wood splitter and his ax to chop logs to four-foot lengths. When orders came in for wood, he loaded the wood into his Chevrolet pickup truck and hauled it to the customers' homes. Each night he gave the information to Alice, and she recorded the number of cords and the price in a notebook for recordkeeping. Poli had learned to write a little, but not enough to keep the books, so the task fell on Alice.

Alice recognized that her husband much preferred working on a farm and in the woods than in a stuffy mill. He definitely was more content, but the only drawback was that he enjoyed a drink with his buddies. Sometimes he came home late and his mood was very unpleasant. Rude comments began to surface after he'd been gone for hours at a local social club. On occasion Alice approached him about this after he had sobered up, and he'd commented that a man needed a time to relax after a long, hard day. She wondered if he had any clue as to how much she worked from early morning to late at night managing their home and growing family. So she prayed diligently each day for strength and wisdom.

One night after having too many drinks, Poli staggered into the house, bumping into chairs. Alice rushed out of their first-floor bedroom and whispered, "Poli, you need to be quiet or you'll wake up the children."

"The children," he drawled, "will be just fine. I work long days and I deserve to go and have a drink once in a while." He plopped into the nearest chair, his eyes glassy and his focus blurred. Alice wondered how he had even made it home.

"It's not the one drink that's the problem. It's having several. You use up money we desperately need to keep these children clothed and fed, keep the house in good condition, and pay our taxes. Need I say more? Consider that the next time you need to be out with the guys. Now, please go wash up and go to bed."

"Stop nagging me. I should just leave this place and see how you like that," he snapped.

"The door is right behind you, Poli, so go right ahead if that's what you want," she said softly. Poli weaved sideways and nearly fell off the chair. Letting her words sink in, he finally got up and headed to the sink to wash his face. Slowly he made his way to the bedroom, removed his clothes, and laid them in a heap on the floor. He slid his legs into his long johns, nearly falling over again. After what seemed like hours to Alice, Poli slid into bed and was snoring as soon as his head hit the pillow.

Thank the good Lord, Alice thought. *Now if only I can go back to sleep. I sure wish he realized how little sleep I get as it is. Dear God, please help me get back to sleep so I can handle what tomorrow will bring.*

The following morning, Poli awakened shortly after dawn and found his wife already in the kitchen preparing breakfast. He said nothing about the night before as he placed a kiss on her cheek. After combing his hair, he walked to the hallway by the back door and put on his hat. In the barn, the cows were bawling so he grabbed the nearest bucket and plunked it down under the first udder. Then he saddled himself on a small stool, warmed his hands before touching the udder of La Noir, and began milking. He could do this with his eyes closed; the rhythm was so familiar to him. He had to keep an eye on the tail and the swiftness of a kick from the old girl.

What a fool I was again last night. How Alice puts up with me is beyond me. I certainly don't deserve a special woman like her. Sometimes I just like being with the guys and forget how many drinks I've had, and next thing I know, I'm drunk. Someone oughta knock me over the head with a two-by-four log and maybe I'd use the sense God gave me. Oh, my head sure hurts this morning. Maybe the children will be quiet for a change. Poor Alice is stuck with them all day long, but she doesn't seem to mind. She just smiles at their crazy antics and keeps on doing her work.

Poli continued the rhythmic tugging on the udders until the first was empty. Carefully he moved the pail away from the "old girl" and set it by the edge of the stall. He moved the stool back against the wall and spoke softly to La Noir. Poli continued to the next stalls and milked the rest of the cows. Once the pail was filled with warm, fresh milk he moved it near the door and placed the stool against the stall door.

Deciding to carry the pail to the house before anyone kicked it Poli lifted it with no effort and walked back to the house. In the kitchen, the children were eating their breakfast of oatmeal and bread. They glanced up at him and giggled as he ruffled their heads on the way to the kitchen counter. Without spilling a drop, he hoisted the heavy-laden pail onto the counter for Alice to strain.

Later on Alice would skim the cream off the top, make homemade butter, and save it in the icebox until needed. Another long day of hard work awaited her. In many ways, having the farm was a blessing as it saved their family a lot of money. On the other hand, it created an extreme amount of work for all of them old enough to help. Joseph was old enough to help his mother with some of the household chores, yet he preferred to be outside playing, as most little boys would.

Chapter Nineteen

ALICE'S ILLNESS

Poli was hired on a construction job and had to be away for several days. Times were difficult for many families, especially those who didn't plant gardens and have homemade canned foods to get through the cold winters.

The brutally cold winter dampened the spirits worse than the summer months as fewer jobs were available and it was difficult to keep warm. Poli had wood to sell, but his neighbors had little money to pay for it. He decided he would join some of the men and travel out of town. He was rugged and could handle the long days required to get the work completed.

At times Alice was left alone with the young children five days a week until Poli returned on Friday night. During one of those departures, Alice became ill. They did not yet have a telephone, so she could not call anyone to help. Her children were too little to send off to get help. As the days wore on, Alice became increasingly weak and was unable to place wood in the stove to keep their home warm.

Alice lay on her bed with a high fever, and her young children snuggled in bed with her under the quilts to try and keep warm. She thought to herself, *I am going to die here in my bed. What will happen to the children? I am so weak I can't even feed them and they keep crying. They are cold, too. Dear Lord, please send someone to help us.* Hours turned into days, and Poli was still away and no one had come.

Odile and Pierre lived only about a mile away and didn't get out much during the winter, and they had young children of their own. They decided they would go pay a visit to Alice since they had not seen her in quite some time. The storm had settled and the sun shone brightly, so they put on their heavy boots and coats and trudged the mile down High Street.

As they were approaching the dark green house, Odile nudged her husband and said, "Look, there's no smoke coming out of Alice's chimney. That's very odd on such a cold day. I wonder what's wrong."

They quickened their steps as much as they were able, holding on to each other's arms as they trudged through the snow up the driveway to the back door. The door was unlocked so they knocked and walked in. The frigid air hit them square in their faces, and they called out, "Alice, are you home?" There was no answer from their daughter so they called out again, louder than the time before. "Alice, Poli, anybody home?"

A moment later they heard a slight murmur from the first-floor bedroom that sounded like one of the children. Pierre Laprise hurried behind his wife as they moved quickly to the bedroom. Alice laid still and the children stirred as they heard their grandparents approach. Little Pete spoke up and said, "Memere, Mama is real sick."

Odile rushed to the side of the bed and touched Alice's brow, feeling the heat. She felt relief that she was alive, but she was concerned about the high fever and what to do with the children. She looked up at her husband and said, "She's alive but has a very high fever. Get the stove going and we can decide what to do next. Look at the ice on the windows. I wonder how long she has been this way."

Pierre rushed to the kitchen stove and placed several large pieces of wood along with small pieces of kindling into the side of the stove and lit a match. He placed the black cast-iron cover back on and hung up the handle. He went back to the bedroom and spoke to his wife. "The stove is heating up. What are we going to do now?" Her eyes filled with tears as she swallowed the lump in her throat.

The children were still cuddled under the blankets, and she didn't have the heart to tell them to leave. It was way too cold for that so she asked them to scoot over to one side of the bed so she could help out their mama. Two of them climbed over their mama, and Odile and Pierre pulled Alice closer to the edge of the bed, trying to wake her.

"Alice, can you hear me? Alice, we're here now. Come on, wake up. Do you hear me, Alice? Don't give up now." Odile rubbed the side of Alice's face as she did when she was a little girl. Alice murmured slightly. "That's it, Alice. Wake up. We are here to help. Your little ones need you."

Pierre left to check on the stove and to see if he could get some water out of the pump, but it was frozen. He took a bucket and went outside and filled it with snow. Taking a large pot, he dumped the snow into it and placed it on the stove to melt. He made two more trips outside until he felt he had enough water for his wife to cook for the children and to treat Alice's fever.

It looked like they hadn't eaten for days, and the youngest whimpered. They were too young to understand why their mama couldn't get up and feed them. He wondered how long Alice had been sick and how long it had been since she'd fed the children. *And where is Poli?* he said to himself. When he was finished, he went back to the bedroom with a wet cloth. The kitchen was warming up, but the bedroom was still cold.

"Where's your papa?" he asked the children.

"He's working far away," said Joseph. "We're so scared, Pepere, and hungry." His soulful eyes stirred a fear in Pepere he'd never felt before.

He swallowed hard and stared down at his worried wife. The baby cried softly, cuddled between Adrienne and Raymond. Pepere moved to the opposite side of the bed and knelt down to speak to his grandchildren.

"I know you're scared, but we're here now and we will get this place warmed up. Memere will take care of Mama. You'll see. Everything will be fine. I'll go check the fire." He got off his knees and rubbed them before heading out the door to the kitchen. *Please, dear Lord, please take good care of Alice. Make her well. Show us what we need to do. Thank You for sending us here. It may have been too late otherwise.*

The kitchen was nice and warm now and spreading into the dining room since he'd left the door open in between. Soon the heat would work its way into the bedroom and he would have the children come out and get warm. Odile stepped up beside him and whispered, "I need to get the fever down, but I also need to feed those little ones. Would you rinse the cloth in cool water to cool her forehead and pour some water into a glass and try to get Alice to drink some? I am going to look and see what food there is around here that isn't frozen solid. Oh, then, could you go get some eggs in the barn please? There should be some in there, the good Lord willin'."

After placing a cold cloth on Alice's forehead, Pepere quickly headed out the back door, taking gentle strides to the barn and being careful not to slip. About six inches of snow had fallen during the night and no one was around to clean it. He had forgotten the basket for the eggs so he doubled back using the footprints he'd made. In the kitchen, he grabbed the basket and hurried back outside. In the barn, he heard a cow lowing and wondered how on earth the neighbors couldn't see or hear that something was wrong.

Reaching under the hens he felt for eggs in the straw. "Oh good, here's one egg," he said to himself and the chickens. "Two, three, four, five, six, seven. Thank you, girls. You are saving the day and you don't even know it. Nineteen eggs today. Thank You, God, for providing for the little ones." The thought of possibly losing his stepdaughter quickened his footsteps toward the nice, warm kitchen.

"Did you find any eggs?" asked his wife.

"Nineteen eggs, dear," and handed the basket to her. "I have to go milk the cows. They are bawling in there. How on earth the neighbors haven't noticed something is wrong, I don't understand." He took a deep breath and sighed.

"Some are quite a distance away and are probably doing their best just to keep warm in their own homes. Maybe the others aren't well either. We can't judge them."

While he milked La Noir (Blackie), his wife was in the kitchen cracking eggs and mixing them in a bowl. Two of the children ventured into the kitchen, tears rolling down their cheeks, followed by hiccups. Memere pulled two chairs out from the table and lifted the little ones onto them, giving each one a hug. "Everything's gonna be just fine. Pepere will bring in some milk in a few minutes, and I will cook up these eggs for you." She gingerly moved their hair out of their faces and caressed their cheeks. "You are very brave boys. Are you warming up now?"

"*Oui*, Memere," said George and Raymond. Their tummies grumbled as they swung their tiny legs off the edge of their chairs. A tear trickled down Odile's cheek as she cracked the eggs, dropping the shells into the sink. Her thoughts returned to Alice. She wondered how long Poli had been gone and how long Alice had been lying in bed sick with her children by her side. *Oh, bon Dieu, we could have lost all of them if you hadn't placed it in our hearts to come today.* Merci beaucoup. *(Thank You very much.) Please give us strength to help them out, and Lord, please heal Alice. Her children need her. Please save the baby she's carrying too.*

"Children, I will be right back. I'm going to check on your mama. You stay here and keep warm okay?" The boys nodded and Memere quietly entered the bedroom with a cold cloth in hand. The bedroom was finally warming up, and Joseph and Adrienne were comforting Edgar. Memere wiped Alice's forehead with the wet cloth and continued down her neck. Alice's clothes were drenched even though it had been freezing in the room a short while ago. *I'd better get her out of these wet clothes and wash her down to get rid of this fever. First, I have to feed the children. Oh Lord, send Poli home quickly please.*

"Children, come with Memere. The kitchen is nice and warm now." Memere picked up seven-month-old Edgar, and the children followed her out of the room. Joseph and Adrienne ran to the kitchen and stood by the stove as they rubbed their hands on their arms. Pepere walked in with a bucket of milk and placed it on the counter. Memere placed Edgar in his cradle and he cried, but she couldn't do anything about that right now.

Memere didn't have time to separate the cream from the milk and decided the children wouldn't mind today. They were too hungry and frightened to care. With the eggs cooking in the cast-iron griddle on one burner, she placed a small pan of water on another and placed a milk bottle in the center to warm up for Edgar. Although she'd had a large family of her own, taking care of these little ones and their sick mother was more exhausting at forty-five years of age. It was certainly not what she expected to find when she and her husband left their home that morning.

The children were so weak they barely spoke. Instead they sat quietly at the table watching her every move. She placed cups of milk on the table for each of them, which disappeared in seconds, the remnants of which lined the shape of their mouths. If the situation wasn't so dire, she would have laughed at the sight of it. She checked the temperature of the milk in the bottle by dripping some on her wrist. *Just right,* she thought.

"Pepere, would you mind feeding Edgar while I finish these eggs?" She lifted the crying baby from his cradle and handed him to Pierre along with the bottle, and he settled in uncomfortably at the end of the table. Odile nearly laughed and said, "He won't break, Pepere. Just place the bottle in his mouth and he'll do the rest." The children giggled and Odile's heart soared with delight. Odile placed two spoonfuls of eggs on each plate and handed them to the children.

"*Merci*, Memere," each child responded as he or she received a plate.

She had never seen them eat so quickly before. "Children, please slow down or you'll get tummy aches and throw up. Eat slowly. There's more on the stove." Halfway through the bottle, Pierre pulled it out to burp Edgar, but he howled. He looked at his wife, unsure what to do.

"You'd better put it back in his mouth or he'll keep crying. Hopefully this one time, it'll be okay." Pierre put the bottle back to the baby's lips, and he immediately quit howling and sucked on it like his life depended on it. Alice usually breast-fed her children, but she was in no position to do that right now.

"More, please, Memere," said Joseph as he lifted up his plate. The others followed suit, so Odile carried the heavy pan to the table and placed one spoonful on each plate and laid the pan back on the burner over a low fire. She wiped her hands on her apron, grabbed a bowl of cold water, and left to check on Alice.

In the bedroom, Alice was sweating and had still not uttered a word. Odile rinsed the cloth in the bowl of water and rubbed it on Alice again, rinsed it and left the cold cloth on her forehead. "Alice, please don't give up. Your family needs you." She left the room again, and found that the children were waiting patiently for more eggs.

"Is Mama gonna be all right, Memere?" asked little Joseph, who had turned around in his seat as he heard his memere's footsteps behind him.

"*Oui, mon cherie,* she'll be fine. Let's say a prayer for her, okay?" They bowed their heads as Odile prayed out loud, "Dear God, You know Mama is very sick. We ask that You make her well again. The little ones need her. We ask in Jesus' name. Amen."

The children responded, "Amen."

Edgar finished his bottle and Pierre lifted him onto his shoulder, patting his back until the baby burped a couple of times. Pierre continued to rub the tiny baby's back until his wife was free to change the diaper. The children finished off the eggs and milk, leaving remnants on their lips and chins. Odile washed their faces and asked them to play quietly.

The children sat on the floor playing while Odile continued to care for Alice and changed Edgar's diaper. Pierre fed the animals in the barn, shoveled a pathway from the barn to the house, and fetched food from the basement for their next meal. Fortunately Alice had canned many jars of vegetables the previous summer. Also in the basement was a large bin of potatoes and some beef in their icebox.

Odile returned to the kitchen and smiled. "Mama has finally woken up. The fever broke too." She took a deep breath and ran her fingers through her hair. The children clapped and yelled, "Yeah!"

Odile laughed at her darling grandchildren. She wondered what her daughter, Alma, must be thinking right now. She had left her with the young children and they had been gone for hours. *She must be worried sick about us. We are never gone this long, especially when it's getting dark out.*

Pierre followed Odile as she motioned for him to follow her into the laundry room to speak with him privately. Once the door was closed, she whispered, "One of us will need to go home and let Alma know what's going on. She'll be worried sick that something has happened to us."

"I've been thinking the same thing. Do you want me to go? Alice is drinking liquids now and seems to be over the worst of it."

"If you don't mind. Otherwise you would need to care for her and the little ones. You and Alma could handle our children easier since they are older, except for Annette, of course, don't you think?"

"True, Odile. I had better get going since it's nearly dark. Will you stay the night with Alice then?"

"Yes, I think that's best. I don't want her having a relapse during the night. Before you leave you should check on the cow and the chickens again. I need to start supper for the children soon."

"Very well, but before I go I will bring some more wood in from the shed so you'll have enough to last the night. I will be back early in the morning with John," said Pierre.

"*Merci*, Pierre."

"No need to thank me, Odile. I'm just happy we came when we did," he said and turned to the kitchen door and headed outside.

Odile walked back into the kitchen and the children turned toward her. Joseph asked where his pepere was headed, and she explained he was getting wood from the shed.

"Petit Pete, you and Raymond watch the little ones for a minute as I check on Mama." Alice was coherent when her mother entered the bedroom and Odile breathed a sigh of relief. "How are you feeling?" she asked as she approached the left side of the bed.

"Tired and thirsty. What has happened and where are the children?" Alice asked as her bloodshot eyes stared at her mother. She hoisted herself up a little against the backboard of the bed. As she did, the wet cloth fell onto her lap.

Odile sat beside her on the bed, gave her a drink of water, and explained. "When Papa and I arrived this morning, you and the children were all in bed together. Your fever was very high and you were not conscious. The children were afraid and some were crying softly. It was very cold as the woodstove was not burning. Don't you remember anything?" She reached her hand to Alice's forehead and although it felt clammy, the fever had not returned.

"Oh, I remember being sick and I could barely move." She touched her head and closed her eyes, trying to replay the events. She continued, "Poli left Sunday night. What day is this?"

"Thursday."

"Thursday? I think it was Monday when I began with a fever and my body ached terribly. I kept up with the wood and feeding the children that day and I think on Tuesday, maybe even Wednesday, I'm not sure. It's a blur. I remember dragging myself to bed, carrying Edgar, and telling the children to come with me. We climbed under the covers and I prayed to God for help. I could hear the little ones crying and talking, but I couldn't move to help them and I dozed off again. It was so very cold in the room."

"The children are fine right now. They ate eggs and bacon earlier, and I will fix them supper soon. Papa will check on the animals once more and then he'll walk home. I'll stay here tonight with you and the children. You get some rest now."

"*Merci*, Mama. I am so tired," said Alice as she fell into a slumber. Odile slipped quietly out of the room and returned to the kitchen to prepare supper. The children played happily and quietly for a short while after supper, and Odile helped them get into their pajamas and tucked them into their beds. She kept Edgar on the first floor with her as she kept vigil through the night rocking by the stove, occasionally refilling the woodstove and checking on Alice.

Odile was exhausted by morning. Edgar awoke with a piercing cry. Odile, anticipating his hunger, had a warm bottle ready on the stove. She checked the temperature of the milk on her wrist, lifted the crying infant from his cradle, and whispered in his ear. He settled down quickly when the nipple of the bottle touched his lips, and he drank intensely for several minutes. Alice appeared in the doorway of the kitchen moments later. And she smiled at her mother and baby.

"*Bon matin*, Mama. Looks like you have everything under control this morning." Edgar glanced at the sound of his mother's voice as she approached the rocker. She was wrapped in a thick robe over her nightgown.

"Good morning to you, Alice. You look much better this morning. How are you feeling?"

"So much better, thanks to you. I don't remember ever being so ill." Her fingers pushed her dark hair behind her ear as she took a seat at the table. "I was afraid for myself and the little ones. How did you happen to come along yesterday with Papa?"

Odile looked into her daughter's eyes and replied, "Papa and I were talking about you, that we hadn't seen you or Poli in a while and felt we needed to come by. The storm had passed and the sun was out so after we shoveled our steps we put Alma in charge of the young ones. We believe the good Lord put the idea in our hearts to come here." She placed her free hand on Alice's and smiled.

"I think so too. It's nothing short of a miracle, because I don't think I would have lasted another day. I have thanked Him many times that He sent you to us. I don't even want to think what Poli would have found when he returns home today."

"Yes, let's not think about that. God decided He needs you here and so do we." Odile lifted Edgar to her shoulder to burp him and returned him to the crook of her arm for the remainder of his feeding.

Alice stifled a yawn, stood up, stretched, and said, "I will get dressed and come back to cook breakfast. The children will be awake soon. It feels good to be up on my feet again." She smiled as she turned toward her bedroom.

*   *   *

Two weeks later, Alice felt strong cramps in her abdomen as she climbed the stairs to the second floor. Her children were getting ready for bed. She stopped halfway up the staircase and held the railing until the pain passed. *What's this? It's too early for labor,* she thought to herself. *I am only four months along.* Later in the evening, the sharp pains returned and continued for hours until she discharged. Alice lost the baby in the wee hours of the morning. She was asleep and resting as Poli made his way out of the bedroom.

Poli worried about the health of his wife, especially after returning home two weeks before to hear the details of her illness. For days, Poli's thoughts of what could have happened tortured him. What if she had died? What if the children had died too? What if Odile and Pierre hadn't showed up when they did? What if Alice survived but had lost one or more of the children? Over and over the questions haunted him until he could have screamed. He placed more wood into the stove as thoughts swirled in his head.

Sitting at the kitchen table around four o'clock in the morning, he wondered how she would take the loss of the one in her womb. Would she blame herself or would she move on and ask the good Lord for help to get her through? All he wanted was for his wife to be healthy again. He ran his long fingers through his short wavy hair.

Someday, he thought, *I will have to install one of those newfangled telephones some of the more well-to-do people have in their homes. That way Alice could call for help when she or one of the children become ill or injured.* With that decision made, Poli quietly exited the house and headed to the barn.

Chapter Twenty

EDGAR: 1931

"Mama, can I go play outside today?" asked Edgar, who would be four years old next month. It was such a beautiful, warm June day and he wanted to be outside with the other children.

"Well, I guess it would be fine for a little while, Edgar. Remember you've been sick for a whole week, so no running around. Make sure you stay close to the house," said Alice.

"*Oui*, Mama," he said as he dashed out the back door. Edgar was tall for his age, looking more like a six- or seven-year-old than a three-year-old boy. His asthma had acted up again this spring with all the flowers in bloom and with his desire to run around the yard.

He soon found Joseph, Adrienne, Raymond, and George over by the barn and ran over to them. They were talking about walking down toward the mills to pick strawberries and surprise Mama.

"Can I go, too?" asked Edgar. "I want to go with you."

"No, Edgar," said Joseph. "You can't come with us today. You've been sick a whole week. Besides, you wouldn't be able to walk that far. It's over a mile away."

"That's right," said five-year-old Adrienne. "Besides, Mama won't let you."

"Can you keep a big-boy secret for us?" asked George, who'd just turned seven a few days before. At their young ages, they felt all grown up just being the oldest of the ever-growing family.

"A secret?"

"Yeah, can you do that? You're almost four years old and growing so big. I know you can do it."

Edgar's sad eyes looked down at his feet and he kicked a few pebbles around with his shoes. When he looked up, he replied, "I guess so, but I really want to go with you, please?"

"Not this time, little brother," said eight-year-old Raymond. "We wish we could, but Mama would not be happy with us. We'll bring back some strawberries for you, okay?"

"Okay," he said with tears forming in his eyes.

The four "big" kids took their pails and snuck under the kitchen window, making sure Mama didn't see them. Papa was in the barn milking the cows since it was early morning. They started walking down High Street toward the mills. Joseph, Raymond, George, and Adrienne laughed, talked, and kicked stones along the way. A few horses and buggies, driven by their owners, went by and the children waved.

By the time they reached the hill going down to Island Avenue, they were warm and sweaty. As they took a break, they heard coughing behind them. They turned around and saw Edgar a few hundred feet behind them.

"Oh no, he followed us. What are we going to do now?" asked Raymond.

"Let's go get him," said Joseph. "It's too far to turn back now."

When they approached Edgar, George asked him, "Edgar, what are you doing following us? We told you it was too far and to stay home."

"I... had... no... body... to... play... with," he said as he took deep breaths.

"Look at you. You're all tuckered out. You'll probably get sick all over again," said George. "Mama and Papa are going to scold us when we get home."

"Well, let's get to the bridge and cross over and find a place for Edgar to rest," said Joseph.

Joseph took Edgar by the hand and they walked down the hill, turned left onto Island Avenue Extension, and approached the narrow boards that acted as a foot bridge leading to the mill yard. The river was high and flowing fast due to the spring thaw. The narrow planks were wet from the morning dew as the children crossed single file on the unstable makeshift bridge. Joseph waited with Edgar for the others to cross, then he gave him strict orders to hold on to his belt and not let go.

Edgar held tight to the back of Joseph's pants and they started slowly crossing the bridge. Suddenly Edgar's shoes slipped on the wet planks and he lost his balance. He let go of Joseph's belt and fell into the cold, rushing water. Joseph screamed, "Edgar," and jumped into the river. None of the children knew how to swim, and the mighty rush of the river dragged Edgar quickly away from them. Joseph tried to grab him but was unable to catch him. He grabbed onto a tree branch and pulled himself on shore. Edgar's eyes were wide with fear as he bobbed up and down in the current.

Joseph yelled to George and Adrienne to run home and get their father. They took off and ran as fast as their young legs allowed as Raymond and Joseph stayed to help Edgar, who was screaming for help.

George and Adrienne never stopped running until they reached home. All out of breath, they ran into the barn yelling for their papa. Papa was milking La Noir (Blackie) when they rushed in. He stood up fast and asked, "What's wrong?"

"Edgar fell in the river by the bridge," panted Adrienne. "Joseph and Raymond are trying to catch him."

"What were you kids doing down by the river?" Poli asked angrily. Fear gripped him.

"Picking strawberries," she cried.

"You two stay home with your mother," he said as his six-foot frame sped down High Street on foot in the direction of Island Avenue.

George and Adrienne ran into the house to tell Mama what had happened. Alice, who had twenty-two-month-old Roland beside her on the floor and was nursing four-month-old Henri with a blanket over his head, listened intently to her two frightened children.

"What were you doing down there?" she asked. "You know you are supposed to ask before you leave the yard."

"We know, Mama. We're sorry," said Adrienne crying even more. "We wanted to surprise you with strawberries." Mama pulled out her handkerchief from her apron pocket and gave it to her daughter. George was crying too. Roland, seeing everyone crying, imitated them. Alice placed Henri over her shoulder and patted his back until he burped. A few moments later he had fallen asleep and Alice placed him in his crib in her bedroom and closed the door.

"Let's pray," she said as she gathered her children in her arms.

*   *   *

Napoleon made it to the bridge quickly and spotted Raymond. He ran toward him and asked where Joseph and Edgar were. Terrified, Raymond said, "Joseph ran by the river trying to reach for Edgar's hand, but he couldn't reach him, and now we can't find Edgar. Oh, Papa!" he cried.

They ran along the Mousam River toward Joseph, who was about a hundred feet away. They dodged tree branches and scrub brush as they approached Joseph. A few neighbors had heard the screams and searched along the opposite side of the rushing river.

"Where's Edgar?" screamed Papa, fear penetrating through his eyes.

"I tried to reach him, Papa, but he kept going down river so fast and I had to go around the trees. Now I can't see him." Napoleon scanned the river and took long strides along the riverbank searching for his young son, swiping his brow with his shirtsleeve, thrashing the branches and shrubs in his path.

By now more of the neighbors plus some of the mill workers arrived, and they were all trying to find Edgar. An ambulance pulled up near the makeshift bridge.

They scoured the Mousam River on both sides until they reached the dam and backtracked toward the tiny foot bridge. When Napoleon was about a hundred yards from the bridge, he spotted a shirt up against the riverbank and heaved the branches away with a mighty force, his heavy boots thumping the ground.

Although he could not swim, Napoleon jumped feet first into the river, gripped the young boy whose clothing had caught onto a tree branch, broke the branch with the force of an angry lion, and heaved the limp body onto the ground. He swiftly yanked himself out of the river and knelt by the boy, trying to revive him. His two eldest boys stood beside him weeping.

*   *   *

Alice paced the kitchen floor and then stopped to look out the west-facing window for the hundredth time since her young children told her the story. She twisted her handkerchief tightly and prayed for her boy like she'd never prayed before. George and Adrienne sniffled and watched their mother. As she looked out the window again, Adri asked, "Are they coming yet, Mama?"

"Not yet." She gave them some cold milk and cookies. She changed Henri's diaper and washed his tiny face. Roland toddled around the kitchen behind his mother as she paced.

She faintly heard the battery-operated clock ticking endlessly in the background. In the distance she saw movement about a half mile away. "*Oh God, please let that be them,* she prayed silently.

George came and stood beside her and asked, "Are they coming?"

"I'm not sure. Someone is coming, but I can't tell who it is." She swiped her wet eyes with her handkerchief and placed it back in her apron pocket and placed her arm around her son's shoulder. Adrienne came and stood on her left.

The figures moved slowly like a slow-motion picture show. Alice recognized the familiar gait of her tall husband. As they came closer, she noticed Poli walking between two boys and holding something small in his hand. She placed her hands on her chest willing herself to breathe. Their heads were drooped, shoulders slumped, and there was no sign of Edgar. *What is he holding in his hands?* She wondered.

As they walked up the gentle slope of the driveway, Alice took the children to the kitchen table. Minutes went by as the back door opened slowly. The boys rushed to their mother's arms, trembling and crying. Poli hung his head and soberly entered the kitchen. He handed his wife two small boots and said, "Edgar's gone" and dropped his tall frame heavily into the nearest chair, his clothes still damp.

"Oh, no, no, nooooooo!" she screamed. *Dear Lord, please help Edgar. He can't be dead. He's not even four years old, Lord. Please bring him back to us,* she prayed silently. Alice wanted to scream again and again but she couldn't. It would frighten her little ones. Tears streamed down her face as she huddled with her young children. Sniffling turned into hiccups. Poli sat with his head in his large, rough hands, muffled sobs penetrating their hearts.

Finally after several minutes had passed, Alice choked out the words she couldn't hold in any longer. "Where is he?"

Slowly Poli lifted his head and looked at her with bloodshot eyes. "I pulled him out of the river and couldn't revive him. He's at the hospital and they will bring him here a little later so we can lay him out. I'll go see the priest later to make arrangements for the funeral."

The children began crying again, all cuddled against their distraught mother. *Dear God, help our family through this please. And take care of our dear Edgar,* Alice prayed silently. *Oh Lord, I'm not sure I can go through this. Please give me the strength to go on, and please take care of the rest of my family.*

Little Roland started crying too when he saw the others crying, and his papa picked him up and held him tightly against his chest.

Later that day, Edgar's body was laid out in the living room for all to pay their respects and say good-bye. Alice often took her handkerchief and wiped the water running out of his nose before people came to pay their respects.

The next day, June 12, the family sat through the funeral in a daze and then watched the tiny coffin being lowered into the ground at St. Ignatius Cemetery, not far from the spot where baby Adrien was buried. Along the left edge of the cemetery were other small crosses depicting the deaths of other babies and children buried in common lots.

So much heartache for so many families, thought Alice as her mind drifted back to 1926.

The blurry images became clear in her mind's eye as she remembered that cold December night. It was snowing hard, accumulating quickly on the frozen ground. Alice was busy caring for her young children, ages five years down to eight months old.

She had made breakfast of homemade crepes, and then scrubbed laundry and hung it on the enclosed front porch. Baby Adrien was getting weaker and she nursed him and checked on him often. Hot soup and bread for dinner warmed her little ones' bellies. Poli had come in to eat two bowls of soup and several slices of bread before heading back out to do chores.

"How is the baby today?" he asked his wife.

"He's getting weaker, like the doctor said last week. I'm not sure he'll make it to Christmas, Poli." She whispered the last part so the children wouldn't hear. They were busy slurping their soup and talking about the snow.

"You'd think there would be something that could be done for him. The doctor has been here several times the past few months."

"I know and I've asked him. He always says we can make Adrien comfortable, but he knows of no cure. It's some form of rupture and it cannot be operated on. We'll just have to keep praying to the good Lord that he won't suffer long."

That evening Alice got the children ready for bed. Five-year-old Joseph wiggled himself into his warm pajamas by the woodstove in the kitchen. Next Raymond, a curly haired four-year-old, mimicked his big brother. Two-year-old George was waiting for his mama to dress him as he played with his pajamas. Alice ruffled his hair and he giggled contentedly.

"Okay boys, time to say your prayers." They knelt and thanks were said. Alice recited the Lord's Prayer and the Hail Mary. "Very good. Now give Papa a hug. It's time to run upstairs." The boys ran up and jumped under the layers of blankets. The air was always cold up there with little heat coming up through the register in the floor. Alice kissed them all good-night and went back downstairs to check on the twins.

She changed Adrienne's diaper and cleaned her face and ears as Adri cackled and squirmed, reaching for her mother's hands. Alice put a warm nightgown and little socks on her baby girl, gave her a big hug, and walked into the bedroom on the first floor. She placed Adrienne in the crib beside her bed and said, "You sleep well, little one. Mama loves you." She draped a few blankets over her tiny body, turned off the lantern, and pulled the door partially closed.

As she entered the kitchen, Poli was holding baby Adrien and softly humming a song. His eyes stared at his sick young son as if to fully embed the image into his mind. His deep hazel eyes looked up and said, "He doesn't look good, Alice. I'm afraid Adrienne will lose her twin brother soon." Alice came over and gently laid her small hand on his large one. He gave the baby a gentle kiss on his head and whispered, "Good night. Papa loves you."

He handed the baby to his mother and got up from the chair and said, "I hate to go, but I need to help plow the roads for a while." Poli bent and gave her a peck on the cheek. He took a chair by the doorway into the hall and put on his boots, coat, hat, and gloves and walked out into the stormy night. They used oxen to pull heavy rollers over the snow so vehicles and buggies with horses could travel.

Napoleon arrived home around midnight to find his weary wife asleep in the rocking chair by the stove holding their infant son. When he approached them, he looked at the baby and knew something was wrong. He felt for a pulse. Nothing. The baby had begun to turn blue.

He shook Alice's shoulder and said, "Alice, Alice, wake up." She awoke, startled to see him standing there and asked, "What? What is it?"

"Your baby is dead," he responded.

*   *   *

A small hand tugged at her dress and Alice was pulled out of her reverie. She wondered how long they'd been standing at the gravesite. She looked down to see five-year-old Adrienne, tears flowing down her face saying, "I'm sorry, Mama."

Alice cradled five-month-old Henri in her left arm and reached down and stroked Adrienne's hair with her right hand and said soothingly, "It's not your fault. It was an accident, Adri."

The priest ended the prayers, and the family and friends walked quietly back to their buggies and a few to their cars. Their silent procession headed back to High Street. As the family consoled each other, they spoke of Edgar's funny ways and smiled.

Alice's mother, sisters, and some of the neighboring women had prepared food for the guests and had it set up on the long kitchen table. Finally, people slowly trickled out a few at a time, once again saying their condolences. All that was left was the immediate family.

The next few days were particularly difficult. The meals went nearly untouched since no one had their appetites. Poli couldn't bring himself to sit at the table. Seeing Edgar's empty chair was too heartbreaking. Instead he chose a chair several feet away and ate in silence.

Chapter Twenty-One

SUMMER OF 1933

Alice was so tired she could barely stand up. Having so many children, cleaning the house, cooking meal after meal, washing loads upon loads of laundry, staying up late in order to catch up on mending was all catching up with her. She prayed silently, *Mon Dieux, please give me the strength to take care of my large family. I am so tired. I am sad, too, because I haven't the strength to play with the little ones and give the others much of my time. You know I love them all and want to do my best, but, God, please help me.* It was about midnight when she slipped into bed. Napoleon was already asleep and snoring. When her head hit the pillow it acted like a dose of sleeping pills as she fell into a deep slumber.

At daybreak the sunshine streamed into the bedroom. Alice prepared herself for another day of hard work caring for her family. She touched her swollen abdomen when the baby kicked inside and wondered what their new addition would be. *Nine children and one on the way,* she said to herself. She breathed in deeply and set about making a huge cauldron of oatmeal. Some of her young ones liked milk in their hot cereal and others preferred it plain. Once the cows were milked by the boys, she separated the cream from the milk for use in making butter.

This June day was particularly warm and Alice wondered what July would be like when her tenth child would show his or her face to the world. *As long as he or she is healthy, that's what matters,* Alice thought. *Poli can't complain he doesn't have any boys—not that he does complain— since seven out of nine children are boys. Well, of course, we lost little Adrien and Edgar- bless their souls-leaving us with five boys and two girls for now. Oh goodness, I hope I'll be able to can the vegetables next month. This little one is due around the time the garden should be ready.* Alice's mind raced that early morning. So much to do, so many children to care for, and the day was gearing up to be hot.

Joseph, who was now called Pete on a regular basis, along with Raymond, George, and Roland, ran down the stairs at 5:00 a.m. ready to milk the cows and check for eggs. Their hair askew, they greeted their mother. "*Bon matin*, Mama."

"Good morning to you, my children. Did you sleep well?" Her dark hair, parted on the left, was pushed back on the right with a long bobby pin. Placing another piece of wood into the stove to prepare breakfast created unwanted heat in the kitchen.

"*Oui*, Mama. I slept good, especially hearing those crickets and peepers singing away," remarked eleven-year-old Pete as he tied on his shoes.

"They sure were noisy last night. I wonder if they ever sleep," said George, who was tall and lanky for a nine-year-old.

Alice's laughter filled the room. "Some time after ten o'clock I hear it get quiet. Then all of a sudden one little peeper will make a tiny noise and all the others join in and make a racket. After a few minutes, they quiet down again just like that." She snapped her fingers. "I think their parents must tell them to go to sleep."

The boys laughed and slapped their thighs.

"That's a good one, Mama. You are so funny," said Raymond, his curls falling across his face as he laced his shoes. "Let's go get the eggs, guys, so Mama can make breakfast." Not noticing the oatmeal, the four boys raced outside, allowing the screen door to slam behind them.

Alice thought, *I suppose I could fix some bacon and eggs as well.*

George returned a short while later with a dozen eggs and dashed to the barn to milk the cows with his father and brothers. Some hens laid early and some later in the morning or early afternoon. Alice shook her head and smiled as she fried fresh bacon on the hot stove, pushing sweat away from her brow with the back of her arm.

Alice's first born daughter, Adrienne, was a petite seven-year-old, and a big help around the house. Setting the table the night before after drying the dishes, she now gently cleaned the eggshells and handed them to her mother. The scent of sizzling bacon and eggs permeated their cozy home. At this time of year Alice always remembered that fatal day two years back when sweet little Edgar drowned in the river. The pain in her heart filled every cell in her body. *God must have needed a little angel in heaven to take precious little Edgar. Mon Dieux, please bless Edgar and baby Adrien and all those who have gone before us.*

"Mama, are you sad?" asked Adrienne, tugging on her mother's blue cotton dress. Alice looked down at her sweet daughter. She didn't want to bring up her sorrow over Edgar since Adrienne had been with her brother that dreadful day.

"Yes, dear, Mama's a little sad, but I am fine. It's very warm today and I am feeling a little tired, too. Now, could you please get me a plate for the bacon? Thank you." She transferred the cooked bacon onto the plate and handed it to Adrienne. The little girl laid it on the table and covered it with a clean cloth. Alice placed more strips of bacon onto the hot fry pan and then flipped the eggs. A few minutes later, Adrienne passed her mother another plate for the eggs.

Running feet rushed through the back door as the boys returned. Quickly washing their hands in the black, cast-iron sink, the boys accidentally splashed water onto the counter and on their clothes.

Within seconds they were seated at the long table. Heads bowed, they sped through grace and dug into their bowls of oatmeal and plates of eggs and bacon. Their tall father came in a few minutes behind them, hungry as a bear after a long winter's nap.

Alice retrieved two-year-old Henri and one-year-old Henriette from their bedroom and placed them on the floor. With so many children and only five bedrooms, they all had to share beds and rooms. Another batch of bacon and eggs was set onto the table closer to her husband, the boys eyeing the plate.

"This one's for me, boys, since I'm bigger than you are and need more food," Napoleon said as he slid three eggs and several slices of bacon onto his plate. Poli ate the most at breakfast and much smaller amounts at the two other meals. Alice opened the oven, removed hot biscuits, and slid them off with a metal spatula. Adrienne stood nearby waiting with another plate as her mother heaped the biscuits onto the plate. She placed the biscuits in front of her father who winked at her and patted her head. Adrienne giggled. Her brothers moaned and rolled their eyes. They were getting too old for pats on the head, so they thought.

Raymond spoke what was on the minds of his brothers and said, "Papa, are you going to share any of those biscuits? We're hungry too, and Mama wants us to pick weeds in the garden."

"Oh, you want some of these biscuits!" he responded with a twinkle in his eye. "Well, I was thinkin' I might bring them to the men who are working in the woods with me today." Raymond's eyes opened wide as he glanced at his brothers.

"Papa, please. Their wives can cook them their own biscuits," piped in Pete.

Napoleon winked at his wife who looked at him over her shoulder as she continued cooking the last batch of bacon and eggs. "Well, I don't know. Those guys sure do work hard out there in the woods." He took another biscuit, buttered it, and took a huge bite. The boys' mouths watered as they licked their lips in anticipation.

"We can muck out the stalls, too, Papa," said four-year-old Roland, who got a kick under the table from his oldest brother. "Ow!"

"What do you mean, 'ow'?" asked Papa.

"Oh nothing, Papa." He knew if he squealed he'd be in more trouble later.

"Well, then, I think Roland has a great idea. After you finish weeding for your mother, you can muck out the stalls. Now you may have your biscuits."

The boys groaned as their hands dropped onto the plate like rain pouring down a gutter. Alice asked them to make sure they saved some for Adrienne, Henri, and herself. She picked up Henriette, took her to her room and changed her diaper. When she returned to the kitchen, she placed her into the high chair and tied a belt around her waist for safety. She repeated the procedure with Henri, warmed a bottle for her one-year-old, and placed a small amount of food for her and Henri on a plate. She and Adrienne sat down to eat as the older boys washed up and sauntered out to the garden.

"Poli, why do you always tease those boys?" asked Alice.

"Me? Tease? Where did you get that idea from?" A not-so-innocent look crossed over his tanned features.

"Yes, you." She smiled at his handsome face. "Don't look at me that way. You know very well what I'm talking about. They'll be awful tired and hot after weeding that large garden. Did you really need those stalls mucked out today?"

"Probably not, but Roland offered." He stuffed the last bite of biscuit in his mouth.

"He's only four years old, Poli. Come on!"

Poli laughed as he slid his chair back and straightened his tall frame. "All right, Alice, I'll go tell them they can clean the barn tomorrow morning. I'll be out in the woods until noon."

"Thank you. Be careful out there."

*　　*　　*

Days of rain followed by several days of sunshine nurtured the soil in the vegetable garden so the produce was abundant by mid-July. The children gathered tomatoes, green beans, and peppers while Alice and Odile cleaned the jars that had been stored all winter in the cellar. Cucumbers, squash, onions, and carrots would be ready later in the season. Soft easterly breezes filtered through the kitchen window, refreshing the ladies who toiled with the large canning cauldron. Quarts of tomatoes and green beans cooled on the kitchen table. Meals of fresh vegetables and bread were the fare during these hot and humid days.

Hours after completing several batches, Alice felt weak and exhausted. Lying on her back on her bed she felt the familiar contractions begin. She tracked the number of minutes in between each one until she recognized the delivery wasn't far off. Alice nudged Poli just before daybreak and asked him to call the midwife. On the twenty-fourth of July, Alice once again gave birth. This time to a little girl they named

Juliette. Juliette was the tenth child born to this hard-working couple. Alice was happy that some of the canning had already been done because a newborn required a lot of time and attention even though they slept a lot in between feedings. In August, Alice and her mother would finish up the canning.

*   *   *

As the weeks passed by, the piles of cut wood grew to over six feet. Poli's sawmill buzzed for hours as he and the boys prepared for the demand of wood for the upcoming winter. He had dry wood piles and fresh wood piles that needed to dry before people could use it for heating. Poli's many customers depended on him to provide wood for cooking and heating.

He'd purchased a twenty-five-acre parcel of backland in High Pine, Wells, where he and the boys and a few helpers cut down trees to prepare a field for cattle and gardening. Months of work at cutting, logging, and pulling up stumps until several acres were cleared was grueling work, especially during the hot months. Blackflies in May and mosquitoes all summer were relentless and left them all with bug bites and welts on their skin. Usually they wore long sleeves and long pants to avoid being bitten and sunburned.

Rocks were piled around the borders forming stone walls. A small barn, erected on the far right corner of the lot, stored the equipment used for farming and would serve as a temporary shelter for the vegetables in the future. At the bottom of the cleared rolling area of land a small, spring-fed brook skirted through the woods. The children enjoyed fishing there on occasion when given time to play.

The owners of the front land had placed a locked gate at the entrance of the narrow right-of-way leading to the acreage to bar the way for trespassers. Poli acquired a key to the lock in order to access his lot.

The right-of-way was bumpy and the children's teeth chattered as they bounced along the path. The scents of dry leaves, wildflowers, manure, and trees permeated the air. Chickadees, finches, bluebirds, crows, robins, cardinals, and a variety of other birds offered a chorus of music sounding through the field and woods. Squirrels and chipmunks scampered about searching for acorns and other delights, burying them in hidden spots below the towering oaks and maples for the long winter ahead.

Peacefulness filtered through the magical air around them once the family sat and rested from their hard chores. At times the children quarreled, and Poli reprimanded them using a tone they understood well. In many ways, the larger the family grew, the harder they worked even with more hands to help. More area was needed for a garden large enough to support the huge family through the winter. Alice became creative in saving time and money and cooking hearty stews and meals. Using resources from their farm far outweighed store-bought items, and the family was able to put money in the bank even during the Depression, which had begun in 1929.

Rationing was common among all the townspeople and throughout the state and the nation. The Alexandres lived off the land as much as possible except for staples such as flour and sugar. Budgeting was an important aspect of their daily lives, and Alice kept accurate records. They had lost some of their checkbook savings when the stock market crashed; however, Pete had saved fifteen dollars, which didn't get swallowed up with the losses suffered by thousands of others. As long as he left it there, he didn't lose it; however, he also couldn't retrieve his funds for nearly two years. The media called that era The Great Depression even though there was absolutely nothing great about it.

News spread that some people had lost everything and some committed suicide because they felt hopeless. Alice felt it a great tragedy when people placed their lives and importance on material things rather than on their Creator and Savior. She remembered their pastor saying that God ultimately has the power to change all circumstances if only people called upon Him. He promised to always provide for the needs of the faithful. Week after week, month after month, they toiled, but they never hungered. Bread-and-butter pickles were canned using cucumbers, peppers, and onions. Carrots were the last vegetable to be canned before the harvesting of the potatoes, which they stored in crates in the cold cellar.

*   *   *

Pete was now attending Emerson School on Main Street. He had attended Edison, Holy Family, and Longfellow School before ending up at Emerson. His siblings also attended a number of different schools.

Autumn boasted brilliant shades of orange, red, and yellow leaves casting their glow over the land. Fallen leaves patted the ground with an array of startling color like a bright colored quilt. The leaves provided added insulation, protecting the ground through the winter while administering necessary nutrients back into the soil. All seasons had their purpose and provided "fruit" for all who labored and toiled.

One day at High Pine the boys began discussing what they had seen the previous autumn during one of their working days at High Pine. Pete had spotted a large moose and had called out to his father. "Look, Papa. Look at that moose. It has two horns instead of a rack."

"Well, if that isn't the darnedest thing I ever saw." Poli removed his hat and scratched his head while staring at the moose over by the tree line. The moose looked in their direction and snorted. "He doesn't look too happy to see us. For now we'd better keep our distance." Raymond, George, Roland, and Henri stood beside their father and brother and watched the moose for a few minutes before returning to their work of clearing stumps. Occasionally they glanced over their shoulders to make sure the moose kept his distance.

Week after week the moose returned and became familiar with the Alexandre boys, so Pete decided to play with him when he had a few minutes to spare. Poli had warned Pete to keep his distance, but Pete being who he was and always getting into some kind of mischief, didn't heed his father's warning for long. As each week passed, he walked closer and closer to the moose until the day came that he stood within a few feet. The moose looked up and then continued to eat without snorting at him. Pete decided he wanted to play with the moose so he conjured up different "games" he could play with him.

Word had spread about the unusual two-horned moose, and eventually people started arriving from all over to get a look at the animal. This interrupted the work Poli and his family were doing at the farm.

During this time, Poli decided to ask the game warden about the unusual moose and the attention it aroused. The warden came by, snapped photos, and suggested Poli charge ten cents a head for people to watch the moose. People arrived from as far away as Massachusetts to see the moose. At times there were so many people on their land, they trampled the meadow so there was no grass for the cattle. The money helped toward the cost of buying hay for the cattle. The moose was large and stood several feet taller than the cows. On one occasion, Poli posed for a photo about ten feet away from the moose.

In the spring, the family would plant corn and other vegetables. Poli built a saw mill at High Pine on the lower portion of the land. "Do you remember that day the moose became angry with Papa and charged at him?" asked George. "Papa ran into the woods and hid behind a big tree."

"Yeah, I remember that. I was so scared Papa would get hurt. Good thing he can run fast," said Raymond. "I wonder whatever happened to the moose. Papa said it took off and the wardens tracked him to Sam Allen Road in Sanford."

"I don't know, but it sure was fun having him around," said Pete. "The part I didn't like was all the people coming. They made the cows nervous and I think the moose got scared of them too."

"Yeah, well, I guess we'll never see him again."

The boys guessed correctly. The moose never returned to High Pine. It was unsure whether he left the area completely or was killed by a hunter. No one ever saw him again.

Back on High Street, the children raked the leaves into huge piles. They'd set their rakes to the side, walk several feet away, and rapidly run and jump into the piles, laughing and squealing. When they pulled themselves up out of the dried and fresh leaves, they sported leaves on their heads and clothing, and some was crumbled into their pockets. The air was more refreshing and the nights much cooler, and the daylight hours were fading away earlier. Autumn was a time of hard work harvesting their potatoes, but it was also a time of having fun in the fresh air before the cold winter would inevitably set in.

The Alexandre children also played with the neighborhood children: the L'Heureuxs, the Lapointes, the Guillemettes, and many others who congregated together at the boys' home. Hide-and-seek, baseball, tin-can alley, and so many other games were played and many bouts of laughter could be heard. They discussed the upcoming winter and how much fun they'd had in the past sliding on their cardboard boxes— sometimes right into the street. They worked hard but they played hard, too, and it helped them appreciate their free time a whole lot more.

Chapter Twenty-Two

POTATOES: 1938

"Potatoes, potatoes, all we eat around here are potatoes," Henri mumbled to himself. Henri sat at the kitchen table with his many siblings, pushing his potatoes around his plate and wishing they would disappear.

"Henri, please eat your potatoes," said his mother as she eyed the young boy from the end of the table.

"But, Mama, I don't like potatoes. Why do I have to eat them? They taste terrible," he pouted.

"Because young boys need to eat so they can grow up strong. Your brothers and sisters are eating their dinner."

"Can't I eat just the meat and the other vegetables? I really, really don't like the taste of potatoes. They feel yucky in my mouth," whined Henri.

"If you eat them with the foods you like, they'll go down easier," said his wise mother.

Six-year-old Henri was not convinced. The conversation around the table turned to the fun things the other children wanted to do outside that afternoon. They discussed snowball fights and building snowmen and forts. The chatter was loud, but Alice didn't mind. She listened and smiled as they carried on about who could build the strongest fort and who could throw the fastest snowball.

"Pete, can I be on your team? Please? You build good forts and throw fast snowballs!" said Adrienne in her singsongy voice. Pete looked at his mother and she gave him a slight nod.

"Oh, I guess so, Adri," he shrugged. "Would you like me to teach you the tricks I've learned to make the best forts?"

"Sure, Pete, would you? I can learn real fast, I promise," said the eleven-year-old to her oldest brother. Her curly dark hair was tied in two long braids, like the Native American girls. Although she was petite for her age, she liked to keep up with the boys since she was the only girl in the first eight children in the family.

Alice nodded her approval to Pete and got up to clear the dirty dishes. As soon as her back was turned, Henri, who was playing with his cold potatoes, scooped up the white mush and dumped them underneath the mittens in the box beside him. He finished his meat, drank his milk, and carried his dishes to the sink.

Henri dashed to the coat hooks by the back door before his mother could question him. Roland, George, and Raymond put on their boots as though they were rushing to a fire. Arms hurried into coat sleeves; hands furiously buttoned coats, pulled on hats, and tugged on mittens as the boys ran out the back door.

Pete picked up the remainder of the dishes and said, "Adri, I'll make sure we wait for you to finish the dishes before we start, okay?"

"Thank you, Pete. The others will probably have half their fort built before I get out there."

"Maybe, but I bet it won't be as strong as ours. Besides, Roland and I will get a head start on ours."

"Mama, are the little children staying inside this afternoon?" asked Adrienne as she dried a plate with a well-worn dish towel.

"*Oui*, Adri, I'll keep them in. They played outside for a while this morning and they need their naps," said Alice as she handed another clean dish to her eldest daughter.

"Good, that way they won't get hurt from snowballs flying everywhere."

Little Henriette heard the conversation and started to cry. "Mama, how come I can't go outside? Henri is small and he's outside," she sniffled.

"Because, Henriette, you are only five and you need to take a nap. Henri took naps when he was five, too. You played out this morning, and I want you and the other small ones to rest and stay warm."

"The big kids have all the fun," she pouted.

"You'll be big before you know it." Once the dishes were done Adrienne washed the table, and Alice slid wood into the stove and washed the faces of her five youngest.

As Adrienne dressed to go out, Alice changed Shirley's diaper and put Henriette, Juliette, Anita, Louie, and Shirley down for their naps.

Outside the older children were building strong forts to protect themselves from the hard snowballs sure to come their way. Pete taught Adri and Roland how to swiftly build a tough fort using hard-packed rectangles stacked on top of each other like a brick foundation. Then he showed them how to fill in the cracks and edges with wet, sticky snow.

Finally both teams had completed their forts and had piles of ready-made snowballs. The January sky was a brilliant, royal blue with a few scattered, puffy clouds floating by like ships sailing on the ocean. The sun's rays beat down on the snow making it sticky, perfect for snowballs and snowmen. The air was a crisp twenty-six degrees; however, the children were warm from many layers of clothing and all the exercise of building.

When they were finished, Pete called out to the other team, "Hey, Raymond, are you guys ready?"

"Ready."

"On the count of three, we'll begin. One, two, three, go!" he shouted.

The snowballs flew back and forth between the two forts, some hitting the tops of their heads, splattering down their faces and necks. The children didn't mind. The more they were hit, the more they laughed.

Some snowballs never reached their targets, but that didn't stop them from trying. Raymond had a good arm so he had Henri and George making the snowballs while he dodged the balls coming from Pete's team and aimed at his opponents. Adrienne and Roland were making snowballs as quickly as they could and were able to use some of Raymond's that didn't break when they flew into their fort.

Alice periodically watched the fun from the kitchen window and giggled each time one of her children was hit on top of his or her wool hat as they all bobbed up and down like horses on a carousel.

They'll be tired tonight, and I'll bet they'll be asleep as soon as they hit their pillows. Alice chuckled to herself. She walked to the pantry to get the flour, lard, raisins, and the rest of the ingredients to make raisin pies, while the little ones slept. Alice's dark hair was pulled back in a bun, and she wore an apron over her brown cotton dress. She wore brown stockings and comfortable black shoes. Although their family was poor, their clothes were always clean and holes and rips patched. Neighbors and family handed down clothing their children had outgrown to help out this growing family.

As Alice made the pies, she wondered how her mother and stepfather were doing. They didn't visit often in the winter since the mile walk was often slippery and the air too cold for their aging bodies. Maybe she would ask Poli to go down and check on them when he arrived home after work. The day reminded Alice of the winter she had taken ill and her parents came to her rescue. A shiver went down her spine as she recalled that dreadful time when she thought she was going to die. She had thanked God so many times since that day that she was alive and able to care for her children.

A couple of hours later, the little ones woke from their naps and came down the stairs to the kitchen, except for the baby. The older children came in wet and happy and telling their stories, their voices loud and excited.

"Mama, did you see our fort? It was the best ever."

"Yeah, we made lots of snowballs and beat Raymond's team."

"No sir, we won!"

"Well, it was hard to count that many snowballs."

"It sure was fun."

"I want to do that again tomorrow."

Alice had a hard time deciphering who said what, they were talking so fast and excitedly, so she responded, "I watched you from the window several times and it looked like a lot of fun."

The coats were hung on the hooks, the mittens and hats placed by the woodstove to dry, and the boots placed on the floor near the coats. The children's hair was sticking up like porcupine needles, their cheeks rosy red like ripened apples.

"Mm, mm, sure smells good in here, Mama. What are you baking?" asked Pete.

"Raisin pies," replied Alice, "for dessert after supper."

"Yum, my favorite," said Henriette.

Shirley began to cry from her crib, so Adrienne went to the bedroom to get her. Shirley stopped crying as soon as she saw her big sister enter the room, her tiny legs kicking back and forth as if to the rhythm of a sewing machine. Adri bent down and lifted the soft child in her arms and hugged her close. The baby giggled and pulled at Adri's lip with her tiny fingers.

"Hey, don't pull my lip out, you silly girl." Adri laughed and Shirley giggled.

Being the oldest daughter was hard work. However, Adrienne enjoyed playing with the babies, tickling them and making them laugh. She carried her small charge to the kitchen where she sat at the table and bounced Shirley on her lap. Some of the other children came over to play with her.

"Hey, baby girl, did you have a nice nap?" chirped Raymond. "Is that your tummy?" he asked as he poked her gently in the belly. Shirley squealed in delight.

Next Henri tried to wash the drool off her face and chin with a wet cloth as she moved her head side to side, avoiding the cloth.

"Hold still, would ya. I'm just trying to clean you up," Henri gently chided. Shirley continued to squirm, and it took every bit of Adrienne's strength to hold her and not drop her to the floor.

"All right, Henri. It's good enough," she said. "She's just a baby and babies drool even if you try stopping it."

Henri shrugged and sauntered off to the kitchen sink, rinsed off the facecloth, folded it, and placed it back on the counter.

"Henri, why don't you clean our boots if you like cleaning so much?" said Pete.

"Yeah, or clean our bedrooms," said George.

"Very funny," answered Henri.

"Boys, since you have all this free time to tease, why don't you go get some wood down in the cellar and fill the wood box for me," said their mother. That comment quieted the boys for a short while as they hauled wood up the stairs a few times and stacked it neatly beside the woodstove.

Alice placed the remaining raisin pies in the oven to bake. She rubbed her lower back as she straightened up. Her belly was swelled with another baby on the way. Alice wondered what this one would be. *I think maybe it will be another boy, since I've had eight sons already. Poli and I better decide on a name soon. It won't be long before this one arrives.*

A few days passed and a terrible odor filled the kitchen. Alice followed her nose in search of the smell. She approached the end of the kitchen table and stared down at the mitten box. Blocking her nose with one hand, she pulled the mittens off the top with the other.

"Ah, the unwanted potatoes!" she whispered.

*   *   *

A week went by and contractions began. Alice knew she needed the midwife. Most of the children were in school and only the youngest ones were at home. She phoned a neighbor to come over and then called the midwife. Mrs. Lapointe helped Alice dress the little ones in warm clothing, and she carried the youngest as they walked to her home. Alice stayed home, got ready for the delivery, and waited for the midwife to arrive. Later that day on January 22, 1938, she gave birth to a healthy little boy whom they named Ronald.

All of Ronald's older siblings hovered around their newborn brother. Although they had many siblings, they never tired of checking out the latest addition to their family. Alice had to gently pry them away and say, "Children, you need to take turns. One at a time so the baby can breathe. Stand in a line and each take a minute to look."

She held fourteen-month-old Shirley in her arms while two-year-old Louie moved forward. He gazed at the tiny infant in his cradle and reached out to touch the tiny fingers and said, *"Bebe."* "Yes, Louie, he's a baby," said his mother. Louie gazed at his brother and whispered quietly. After a minute or so, she said, "Okay. It's Anita's turn now. Louie, come next to me." Louie stood beside his mother, holding on to her leg while three-and-a-half-year-old Anita peeked into the cradle.

"Mama, how come he doesn't have hair?"

Alice laughed and said, "Not all babies are born with hair. Many come out bald and then the hair grows in later."

"Did I have hair?" asked Anita as she stroked the little arm sticking out of the blanket.

"Hmmm, let me think," said Alice as she rubbed her index finger along the side of her cheek. "Yes, I think you had a little bit of hair, Anita."

"That's good." She sighed with relief. She moved away to allow five-year-old Juliette to come forward. She whispered to the baby and stroked his head, then ran off to play. Next in line was six-year-old Henriette, followed by seven-year-old Henri. Each had questions about their new brother. Roland, Adrienne, George, Raymond, and Pete each took their turns, greeting their brother and telling him about games they played or, to tease one of their siblings behind them, telling the baby to watch out for the next one in line because he was naughty.

Alice put a stop to it before a fight ensued and said, "Boys, that's enough teasing now. Go off to play outside. Supper will be ready in an hour or so. Adrienne, I need your help with setting the table."

Outside the snow was thick and the older boys made snowballs and chased each other around the yard, sinking through deep snow and struggling to get away from flying snowballs. Soaked to their knees an hour later, they trudged through the back door, pants dragging on the floor from the moisture. Alice took one look at them and clicked her tongue and said, "You hurry on upstairs and get out of those wet pants and socks. Then go hang them on the racks in the cellar. And please don't drip all over the floors."

"*Oui*, Mama," they called over their shoulders on the way up the staircase, closing the door at the bottom to keep the cold air from filling up the kitchen. Upstairs it was so cold they could see their breath. The boys hurried out of their wet clothing, quickly slid into their dry clothes, and ran back down the stairs lugging their drenched belongings in a ball. They crossed the kitchen into the washroom, opened the cellar door, and pounded down the wooden steps in their stocking covered feet. Papa had installed a furnace after many years of using only wood; however, there was still a woodstove beside it that dried the laundry hanging on the rack. They draped the wet clothing over the rungs and rushed back upstairs to eat supper.

Papa returned from a day of loading wood into his truck and delivering the cut and split wood to families living downtown. He was tired and hungry and his children made room for him to wash up before settling into their seats.

After finishing their stew and bread along with raisin pie, the boys were dismissed. Some of the older ones headed outside to help their father in the barn while the young ones played. The older girls helped clear the table, wash and dry the dishes, and place them carefully into the white clapboard cabinets. Once the children were in bed for the evening, Alice took out her mending and darned socks, repaired pants, and sewed buttons on shirts. Other times she embroidered or knitted while keeping the woodstove going through the night, often falling asleep in her rocker. She crocheted doilies for the dressers and dresses for dolls. The long flowing dresses spread out and the dolls stood up as a type of centerpiece on their beds.

With many hands to help with outdoor and indoor chores, the work was somewhat easier in some ways, yet in many ways feeding a huge family and mending their clothing was burdensome. Alice recalled one day when Poli wasn't home and the responsibility of slaughtering a chicken for a meal fell upon her. Outside she'd found the ax and placed it by the chopping block. After a time running around trying to catch a chicken, she finally captured one and carried it to the block. She managed to chop its head off and the remainder of the chicken ran all over the yard, spewing blood all over before succumbing to its death. Alice was so frightened from the incident she decided right then she would never again butcher a chicken.

Chapter Twenty-Three

YOUNG ROLAND: 1939

At the age of six, Roland had attended Lincoln School in Springvale village, in the town of Sanford. He was sent there rather than Holy Family School because the school was full. Later he was sent to Hamlin School in Springvale, and then he went on to Holy Family. At the age of ten, he often complained to his dear mother that the Catholic school gave too much homework. She chuckled. Most of her children were not fond of homework.

Roland loved the outdoors, especially fishing, and he worked in the woods alongside his father. His other chores were to take care of the cows and the chickens. Sometimes, things upset him so he'd threaten to move away from home.

On one particular day, as Roland walked into the house he was peeved, and his mother took note. His older brothers were being mean to him and he was tired of them. He was also very tired of all the chores he had to do. He slammed the door and went upstairs to his room, where he gathered his few possessions and placed them in his handkerchief and tied a sling to it. When he came downstairs, his mother was in the kitchen, and she could tell he was still upset.

"I'm leaving," he said in a huff as he swung the sling over his shoulder.

His mother said, "You are? What's wrong this time, Roland?"

"I don't want to talk about it. I'm just tired of all the work I have to do, and the boys picking on me, so I'm running away."

"I see. I'm sorry you feel that way. If that's what you really want to do…" She left the sentence unfinished.

Roland left the house and walked out behind the barn and up the hill. His mother watched where he was headed and saw him sit at the top of the hill. Behind the hill it was all wooded, and she didn't think her young son would venture further than that. He needed time to cool off.

Louie asked his mother, "Mama, why is Roland running away? What's he so mad about?"

"Oh, I don't know exactly. Your big brothers were picking on him and sometimes they don't know when to stop."

"Will he come back?"

"Oh yes, Louie, he'll be back. Don't worry." She patted the little boy's head.

To herself she said, *He's afraid to go into the woods alone and it will be dark soon. Besides he'll be hungry. He'll be back to eat.* She peeked out the window occasionally to see if he was still on the hill, and then she went back to preparing supper for the family. The other children had been outside playing, except for the youngest who she kept near her.

Alice fed her family and answered their questions as to why Roland wasn't there. They were puzzled as to why he'd want to run away and not come home for supper. The older sons thought it quite funny that they were able to get him so annoyed. Sometimes they could be rather malicious.

Up on the hill, Roland remembered the stories his parents would tell about "Loup Garou" who roamed around in the woods and came out at night around seven o'clock. Loup Garou was a werewolf who didn't like children, so the saying went.

The sun was going down and Roland was becoming more and more nervous, and his stomach growled like that mysterious werewolf. The night sounds began, which made the boy fidgety. Every sound made him jump as he looked around expecting to see Loup Garou. Roland decided to start his way back toward the house. He gingerly walked down the hill and climbed on top of the shed roof. He waited a little while longer for the coast to be clear. It was getting darker and darker, and Roland was getting more anxious about Loup Garou coming out of the woods and eating him.

He jumped down from the roof and walked across the gravel driveway toward the back door of the house. His mother saw him coming and smiled. He came in the back door and into the kitchen still carrying the sling over his shoulder. His head was bent and he stared at the floor.

"Are you hungry, son?" his mother asked.

"Yes," replied the wayward son.

"Good. I'm happy you came back home." She had a plate of warm food ready for him and placed it on the table. Roland quickly devoured his meal without looking at his mother who sat in her rocking chair knitting. Once finished, he washed up at the kitchen sink and went upstairs to bed, exhausted. His mother smiled and knew he'd do it again, for this was not the first time. Roland had run away in the same fashion many times, but he had never ventured further than the hill behind the barn.

Chapter Twenty-Four

1940

"Mama, what's your favorite flower?" asked Juliette one hot summer day as she and her mother were outside in the vegetable garden gathering tomatoes, cucumbers, green beans, and scallions into a large bowl.

Alice gazed around the yard, at the flowers growing around the edge of her house. She brushed a strand of hair away from her face with the back of her arm. Sweat poured down the side of her face as the sun beat down upon her skin. "Although I enjoy all kinds of flowers, my favorite is the gladiola. Their colorful heads make me smile, especially when they have several blooms on them. See over there by the window how pretty they are in the sun?"

"*Oui*, Mama, they are very pretty. I like all the colors too. I like yellow, pink, lilac, baby blue, and green. I like summer because it has lots of color," stated the seven-year-old. "But what about the roses, Mama? Why do roses have thorns? They hurt when they prick my fingers." She looked at the tips of her fingers as if remembering the blood drawn from touching the prickly stems.

Alice laughed. "Juliette, I do not know why God gave roses thorns. For that matter, I don't know why He put thorns on raspberry bushes either. Maybe someday when we're in heaven we'll be able to ask Him. Let's finish up out here because it's awful hot and Shirley, Ronald, Andre, and Roger will be waking from their naps soon."

"Oui, Mama." For the next ten minutes, mother and daughter were alone with their thoughts. Alice pondered how she had been able to manage having fifteen babies, losing two little ones, suffering two miscarriages, and having the strength to maintain the home.

Only by the grace of God, she decided. *Lord, I'm forty-one years old and not sure how many more pregnancies I can endure.... Andre was born last year and then last month Roger was born. Please give me strength and keep me alive long enough for all these children to reach adulthood. What would Poli do with such a brood all by himself? The children would probably be separated among the relatives. No, that won't do at all. You'll have to keep me alive, that's all there is to it.*

"Let's go inside now, Juliette. We have enough vegetables for now and the rest will ripen soon." Alice raised herself, brushed the dirt off her knees, and hoisted the bowl onto her hip as she followed Juliette down the narrow row toward the house.

Alice and her two elder daughters, Adrienne and Henriette, washed the vegetables in the cast-iron sink prior to cutting off the ends of the beans and slicing the cucumbers and tomatoes for their noon meal. The day was so hot that their appetites had lessened. Alice and her children gathered to eat fresh bread and vegetables after saying a quiet grace.

Poli had taken his dinner, packed in a black box, into the woods with him early that morning and wouldn't return until the supper hour. He and his men, including his older sons, stayed busy logging trees. Alice always packed him plenty of food, and most days he returned with one sandwich still in his box. As soon as he'd arrive, the children at home would ask if he had anything left from his dinner, hoping it was their turn to receive the treat. With a twinkle in his eye, he would tease them, keeping them in suspense.

On this particularly warm summer day, Poli arrived earlier than usual, entered the back door, and removed his heavy work boots. Before he entered the kitchen, he could hear the children whispering as they tried to guess whether or not he had any of his food left. He took his time approaching the table and glanced up at his wife at the further end of the room. Several years ago he had removed the wall separating the small kitchen from the dining area to make it one long room to accommodate a larger table for their enormous family. She smiled a knowing smile and winked as the children gathered around their papa.

"*Bonjour*, Papa, did you have a good day at work today?" asked nine-year-old Henri as he eyed the black box on the table in front of his father. Roland and Henriette nudged him in the ribs, so he continued, "Do you have any food left in your box?"

Poli had a hunch his children put Henri up to it, and while trying to recall whose turn it was, he scratched his head and said, "Well, what makes you ask such a question, Henri?" hoping his wife would give him a clue. She was great at remembering such things as this; however, she wasn't looking in his direction.

"Well," Henri said as he turned to look at his siblings hovering beside him, "'cuz sometimes you don't eat all your food and... and... you sometimes share with us. That's all." He quickly added the last two words and let out a breath.

Poli suppressed a laugh since he knew his boy was frightened to ask. He slowly lifted the lid on the box and peeked inside as if he didn't know for sure there was anything in there. He glanced at all the young faces around him and wished he could hand each of them a morsel, but it was not possible. There were too many mouths. He caught Alice's eye and she nodded toward Henriette and shrugged her shoulders. Oh how Poli wished he could understand what that gesture meant. Did he give his half sandwich to his daughter (who obviously put her younger brother up to the task of asking) or did he give it to Henri?

"Hmmmm, I guess I do sometimes share what's left, don't I? Well, I wonder whose turn it is to get something—that is, if there is something left in here. There might be a half sandwich," he said as he reached into the box. "Would it be you, Henri? Is it your turn? I forget these things." Henriette's eyes widened and Poli wondered if she'd speak up or wait until Henri answered his question.

Henri turned toward his sister, fidgeting with the edge of his shirt, as though he was in a quandary as to what he should do. Eyeing the half sandwich in his dad's hand, he swallowed hard. Finally, he blurted out, "No, it's not my turn; it's Henriette's turn, but she made me ask you." Henri looked toward the floor.

"I see," said Poli. "Well, then, this is what I'm going to do." All the children waited for his decision. Even the three eldest boys who'd come in the back door. "Since it is Henriette's turn and since Henri was made to ask the question, I am going to split this half sandwich into two pieces so you can each have some. How does that sound?" he asked as he cut the sandwich in two and held the halves toward his children.

Tears sprung to Henriette's eyes as she swallowed and whispered, "That's okay, Papa," and reached out to take her piece. Poli handed the second half to Henri, who smiled gratefully and ate it quickly as though his father would change his mind. Poli suppressed another laugh and stood to wash at the kitchen sink before supper. Pete, Raymond, and George followed behind him to clean up from their day in the woods. They rarely returned home with food left in their dinner boxes.

The children ran outside to play ball in the yard with their homemade bats and ball, placing "bases" around the driveway and making their own rules. Poli's wood saw sat to one side of the tall pile of logs and the children stayed away from that area. They focused their attention on having fun as their suntanned skin warmed in the hot sun. Friends soon arrived to join the lively group, and for the next hour they merrily ran bases, chased balls, and threw toward home base laughing hysterically. About five o'clock, Adrienne called outside to say that supper was almost ready and for the children to come in and wash up.

Their friends left and the boys and girls put their bats and ball in the barn until the next time. Poli and the older boys finished the milking and returned to the house. The youngest were fed first. Poli and the boys ate next, followed by Alice and the girls as there wasn't enough room at the table for all of them to sit at one time. With supper completed, the girls helped their mother clean off the table and wash the dishes while the boys took care of the outdoor chores, caring for the animals and chopping wood.

Once all the children were in bed, Poli discussed the issue of the sandwich with his wife. "Did I understand your nod correctly that it was Henriette's turn to get my sandwich or had she been naughty today?"

Alice lifted the cup of tea and took a sip before answering. "She had been naughty today. She had been teasing Henri and some of the younger ones and bossing them around. It was her turn, yet I was glad you gave only part of your sandwich to her and gave the rest to Henri. She had put him up to asking because she knew she'd been in trouble earlier. Sometimes she acts like the boys and gets a little rough with Juliette, Anita, Louie, and Shirley so when Henri tries to stop her, she turns her attention to him. I've tried talking with her about this and she promises she'll stop, but I catch her doing it again a day later. Maybe you should talk to her."

"I will talk with her after work tomorrow. There is no need for her to behave like that. She definitely is a tomboy. She'd rather milk a cow than help you in the house." He chuckled and shook his head.

"That's true. I cannot seem to get her interested in sewing or washing dishes or cleaning the house. She finds excuses and asks if she can do something in the barn instead. She would much prefer grabbing a pole and a line and go fishing with the boys. It's not fair to leave the burden of the household chores to the other girls. There's so few of them compared to the number of boys we have."

"We do have a bunch of boys and some are quite rambunctious. Too bad we didn't have a few more mild-mannered kids," said Poli.

"I think they take after you and that's why they are so rambunctious, so you have no one to blame but yourself," said Alice with a mischievous smile.

"Oh, so I am to blame for their mischief. I do recall there are times you play your little pranks on them so very innocently. I know you play that game with the blankets. The one your mother played with you when you were a child. How when you slowly walk up the stairs and out loud say 'one step, two steps,' and so on while the kids are in their beds, and then you pretend you can't find them until you check their beds and lift one blanket and the second as you recite the words 'one blanket, two blankets,' and so on. Then the children are squirming and giggling with anticipation. So don't think you can place all the blame on me, young lady."

Alice laughed. "Young lady? These days I certainly don't feel very young. Anyway, what about you with all your childish pranks especially on April Fools' Day? How many times have you tricked them and me on that day each year? Or the time I was miscarrying and you heard Juliette and Anita running toward the woods to find you, and you hid behind a tree. Your worker had no idea where you disappeared to when they asked where you were. It wasn't until they said I was in trouble that you came out. No, no, you cannot get out of this one, Monsieur Alexandre."

"Well, maybe we are both to blame for the naughtiness in our children or maybe we can blame it on the Indians who drop them off here." He laughed at their ongoing joke of telling their children that the newborns arrive by the Indians, so they didn't have to answer their questions about where babies really come from.

They laughed until their sides hurt. Finally after catching her breath, Alice said, "Shhh, we're going to wake up the children." Moments later Andre began to cry, so Alice got up from the table and said, "See what I mean? Now I have to feed this one before I get ready for bed." Alice gently tapped her husband's shoulder as she brushed past him.

After supper the following evening, Poli asked Henriette to join him in the barn. Sensing something was wrong, Henriette searched the faces of her siblings while tying her shoes. Nothing about their expressions gave her a clue as to what Papa was going to talk to her about so she tried to relax. After all, wasn't being in the barn better than helping clean dishes? she thought to herself. The eight-year-old child, braids bouncing, hurried behind her father so as not to upset him. She prayed he wasn't angry over something she had done. *Maybe Mama told him about yesterday,* she thought. *If she did, I'm in big trouble with Papa.*

Poli opened the door to the first stall, stood back to allow Henriette to enter ahead of him, and closed the door behind him. Henriette knelt near the newest calf, hoping Papa would soften a bit if he was indeed angry with her. She heard the weight of his heavy boots on the hay beside her. She stood and gazed up into his face. Sometimes it was difficult to decipher his mood. Today she had no idea what was on his mind, so she stood and waited.

Poli cleared his throat and began, "Henriette, Mama told me about yesterday. She also said that you pick on the younger children quite often, sometimes bullying them. What do you have to say for yourself?"

He leaned his strong frame against the nearby post, folded his arms across his chest, and waited.

Henriette gulped and cast her gaze on the floor. She knew she couldn't lie because she was sure to get a whipping; however, she was unsure how to answer him.

"I'm waiting, Henriette."

"Um, well, I don't know. I was naughty. I shouldn't have picked on the kids, I guess. Sometimes they get in my way and I get mad."

"Hmmm, is that all you have to say? Seems to me that this kind of behavior has been going on for quite some time now, and Mama has asked you to stop many times. I know you are only eight, but for an eight-year-old you can be pretty mean. The others are just little children and they need to be taken care of, not hurt."

"*Oui*, Papa. I'll try to do better. I just like playing with the boys and working in the barn with the animals better than helping Mama with the children. Then she makes me stay in and clean the table and change diapers and I don't like it."

"Your mama has a lot of work to do and she needs help. Adrienne can't be the only one helping in the house. She works over in the mills and is tired at the end of the day. You're the next oldest girl, so a lot of the work does fall on you. Juliette and Anita do a little bit, but they are only seven and six years old. I need you to think about this before you decide to bother the children again. I want you to help Mama more than you have been. She is tired. She is up late at night and gets up early in the morning. Now I don't want to hear from her again that you are giving her trouble, do you hear me?"

With her head bowed, she answered, "*Oui*, Papa."

His large hand patted her on the head as he said, "That's a girl. Now, go on up to the house and see what still needs to be done. And, Henriette, mind that tongue of yours."

Henriette let out a breath and then dashed out the door her papa had opened, thankful she hadn't been hit with a switch on her backside. Mama looked up from her rocking chair as she entered the kitchen. Roger was asleep on Mama, so she approached quietly.

"What do you want me to do for you, Mama?" she whispered.

Alice smiled and whispered back, "I'd like you to take over drying the dishes since Juliette has done half of them already. Juliette's towel looks very wet, so get a dry one. I will put Roger to bed now and I'll be back in a minute."

Henriette slid the drawer open and retrieved a clean, dry towel and began drying the remainder of the dishes. Juliette scampered off to play with Anita and Louie in the corner of the kitchen. Henriette knew she got off easy this time and had better be careful tomorrow and the next day and the day after that or else Papa may not be so easy on her the next time.

Mama returned to the kitchen and said, "You're doing a good job, Henriette. Just set the dishes on the table like we usually do and put the rest away please. After that, you may go play until it's time for bed."

"*Oui*, Mama. *Merci*."

"You're welcome."

Out in the barn, Poli laughed out loud once his daughter was out of earshot and before the boys were due to come in and milk the cows and wash the walls. *She looked so scared I thought I'd burst out laughing with*

174

her here, he thought to himself. *She does need to control that tongue of hers or else she's going to get into a heap of trouble later on. I wonder why she hates housework so much?*

Poli scratched his head and replaced his cap, trying to remember if any of his sisters or aunts ever hated household chores like his daughter. *She sure is a tomboy. Hopefully she'll outgrow that someday. She just might give her future husband a run for his money. Or maybe she'll become a nun.* He laughed even harder at that thought. *I could just see her asking Mother Superior if she could go fishing or milk a cow!* He howled again causing La Noir, the barn cat, to scamper off into the rafters above.

In the evening, Poli told Alice that he would be going to work using his bulldozer in Massachusetts. "They need strong men and the bulldozer to build new roads and highways. The older boys can come with me. We need the money, but you'll be alone during the week."

"You and the boys will be gone all week and returning on the weekends?"

"Yes, it would be too expensive to travel back and forth, so we will rent rooms. The men who are hiring said there are some older couples who rent rooms in their homes to help with their expenses. They provide meals and clean the rooms. We could double up in the rooms to save money."

Poli studied his wife's face and noticed that she was thinking it through before responding. He learned a long time ago that she didn't react quickly but it took her time to think before speaking. He stood up to get a cup of coffee, stirred in a little cream, and sat back down at the table beside her.

Finally she spoke and asked, "Do you really think it's necessary? I mean, you have the wood business and the animals to care for. Will the pay be worth it to travel that far and be gone from home that much?"

"Yes, the money will definitely be better than what I'm bringing in now. With so many mouths to feed and clothe, our income is stretched, as you know very well."

"How many weeks do you anticipate this going for?" Alice asked as she darned another sock.

"That depends on how well we work and the weather. It may be a couple of months or more if they hire us on for more than one project. I know it will be hard for you here with the girls and only Roland and Henri to help with the outside chores, and with the small children to care for, but please think about it."

"I promise I will think and pray about it."

A couple of weeks later Poli, Pete, George, and Raymond left for Massachusetts to begin road construction. Alice worked hard and, although the time seemed to go by quickly during the week, in some ways she felt more tired. On one hand she had four less mouths to feed so that was a savings in food, money, and work. On the other hand, the barn chores along with the gardening, cooking, and cleaning had to be spread out among less people, so the burden increased for each person.

Pete was now nineteen, followed by Raymond at eighteen and George at sixteen. They had interests in girlfriends, so on weekends when they were home, they spent time with their female friends. Raymond had a particular interest in Florence Woodman, and Alice thought there may be some wedding bells for them in the not-so-distant future.

* * *

"Mama, Mama, fire, fire!" screamed Henri from the front porch. Alice's heart beat wildly as she rushed toward Henri's voice. Across the street, flames and black smoke billowed from the Genests' home. Alice unlatched the screen door and told the children to remain in place. As she ran across the street, Madame Genest dashed out her front door, her clothes on fire as she let out a blood-curdling scream.

Alice yelled back toward her house, "Henri, bring me a blanket, quick!" Henri ran into the house and grabbed a blanket off his mother's bed and ran out the front door toward his mother. Alice grabbed it, ran back toward the screaming woman, and wrapped it around her to extinguish the flames. Soon several neighbors gathered around; they asked if the children were in the house. Madame Genest nodded her head and the men rushed to find the children. The children ran out from the back side of the house.

Madame Genest was in tremendous pain and she screamed and moaned, delirious and thrashing around. Alice spoke to her gently to try and calm her. She knew her dear neighbor was in tremendous pain from the severity of the burns.

The fire truck and ambulance barreled down the street and stopped in front of the house as neighbors moved out of the way. The ambulance attendants took charge of Madame Genest as Alice explained that she had been engulfed in flames and that her children were out safely. Madame Genest had yelled something about gas. The firefighters worked furiously to combat the blaze and to hose down the houses on either side so they wouldn't burn down too. The male neighbors filled buckets of water and threw the water into the flames.

Madame Genest's burns were severe, and when Alice inhaled the horrid smell of burned flesh, it engulfed her and she almost lost her breakfast. She gazed often at her home to make sure her children remained on the porch. They stared at all the commotion, eyes wide open. Some cried, but they stayed there watching. Once Madame Genest was hoisted into the ambulance and taken to the hospital, Alice prayed for her as she slowly, shakily walked across the street to her home and family.

She wrapped her children in her arms as they stood watching helplessly as the firefighters worked feverishly with the neighbors until the flames were extinguished. Their bodies and clothing were covered in black soot as they stared at the charred home. After a time, Monsieur Genest arrived home. He ran toward the crowd, yelling for his wife and children. Alice again asked the children to remain on the porch or go into the house as she ventured across the street.

The men told the distressed husband that his wife was badly burned and was taken to the hospital. One offered him a ride. He turned to look at Alice as she approached the crowd and he said, "The neighbors said you put the fire out on my wife. Thank you." He choked on his emotions.

Alice responded, "You're welcome. I did the best I could. If you want, I will take your children to my home so you can go see her at the hospital." He nodded and walked over to his children and told them to go along with Madame Alexandre and he would come fetch them when he returned from the hospital. A couple of them wanted to go with him to see their mama, but he gently told them they couldn't. He turned toward his neighbor and followed him to his truck. Alice led the children across the street as they whimpered silently. Two of her neighbors followed her into the house.

The women helped soothe the children by getting them something cool to drink and some cookies to eat. They had so many questions about what happened and where their mama was and where they were going to live. Alice and her friends did their best to answer and comfort them, but they didn't have all the answers. They spoke among themselves later as to where the family would live. The women said they would discuss this with their husbands and neighbors and come up with some type of plan.

Later that day, they were notified that Madame Genest died from her burns. Alice and her family and their neighbors assisted Mr. Genest and his children by finding them a temporary home, bringing meals, and caring for the younger children. The children wept often in the first days, but as time went on, the healing process began. All the neighbors were deeply distraught at the loss of their friend; however, they all pulled together as a community to help the grief-stricken family.

Chapter Twenty-Five

WAR: 1941—1943

Although the Great Depression ended, there were still many people who barely had enough to eat. Poli and Alice were very thankful their garden had done well throughout the summer. The canned goods would last through the winter and so would the butchered meat they stored in their shed and in their meat locker on Main Street.

A few weeks back, several of the men gathered at a neighbor's property to butcher their animals and prepare the meat for the winter. This was an annual event, and the location rotated among families in the group. With so many hands at work, the process took less time than each man handling his own butchering. The men used boiling water to remove the hair from the animals, and then they prepared the meat for freezing. They rented lockers at a facility across the street from Breton Avenue where the freezers kept the meat from spoiling.

The Alexandre family raised cattle, pigs, and chickens. Alice made blood sausages and separated the cream from the milk to make butter. Juliette did not like stirring the cold blood to make blood sausages; however, they all had to pitch in and help. Some of their meat was hung in the shed, where it stayed cold all winter; however, they also bought ice from an ice truck for ten to fifteen cents a pack until they were able to buy a refrigerator.

Poli's logging business helped provide enough wood for their household as well as for many families in the Sanford region. In the winter, he worked as road commissioner using oxen to pull a roller to pat down the snow in the roads to make it passable for vehicles and horses. He led a team of men who maintained all the roads in Sanford and Springvale.

In the evening, Poli listened to his battery-operated radio to hear the news, music, and talk shows. World War I had ended in 1918. In 1939, Germany invaded Poland on September 1. Two days later, Britain and France declared war on Germany. Within a month, Poland was defeated and was partitioned by German and Soviet forces. Threats and rumors of another world war filled the airwaves. A man named Adolf Hitler had taken leadership in Germany, and surrounding countries feared the rumors building up about him. The Japanese were also taking over islands and pushing their way through nations. The United States of America didn't think they'd be a target, especially with a large military.

Night after night, Poli listened for updates and wondered how it would affect the United States of America and whether or not they would get involved in stopping the evil in Europe. Rumors of horrible prison conditions, gas chambers, and mass murders ran rampant throughout the country for two years. Newscasters reported that millions of Jews were being pulled out of their homes and businesses by the Nazi regime and packed onto trains—and never heard from again.

Alice and Poli prayed for Europe and prayed the United States wouldn't have to get involved, but they knew something had to be done. The United States was a superpower and had a military strong enough to help defend these nations against the evil powers. The Russians were attacking Europe from the east, and some of those lucky enough to escape the Nazis found themselves in the hands of the Russian army. Some were killed and others imprisoned. People fled from Germany, Poland, Norway, Belgium, and other surrounding regions to safe havens as far away as Cuba and the United States.

On December 7, 1941, the family's fears became reality when news of the Japanese military, an Axis power, bombed a US military base at Pearl Harbor, Hawaii. President Roosevelt's wife, Eleanor, made the announcement during her usual Sunday address to the nation. It was the first time a First Lady ever addressed the nation on a topic as devastating as war. The United States immediately declared war on Japan. Four days later on December 11, Germany and Italy declared war on the United States.

Poli feared his eldest sons would enlist or be drafted into war now that President Franklin D. Roosevelt had declared war against Japan. Would his sons get involved with the conflict in Europe or be sent to the Pacific to fight the Japanese? Night after night he and Alice prayed for the world, the innocent people getting killed, and the families left behind to bear the grief. They prayed for the war to end quickly. The world seemed to be going mad—so much killing, too much greed and hatred.

After the children had gone to bed, Alice and Poli discussed their fears quietly. They knew that Pete, George, and Raymond had heard the news because they were young adults. Adrienne, at fifteen, worked in the mills so she was also aware of it. However, they tried to keep the horrible news from the younger ones. At some point it was inevitable that they would find out. Men would be called into service by their president. Neighbors, family, and friends would be drafted to fight against the evils of the world.

One evening, Alice confronted Poli about her fears. They lay in bed, speaking softly about the latest news. "Poli, I need to speak with you about Pete."

"Pete? What about him?"

"I've seen that look in his eyes lately. You know the one I mean? The one where he gets an idea and he's bound and determined to get his way? I've seen that look just before he has taken crazy chances."

"Oh, I know that look. Like the time he slid down the hill on that piece of cardboard and ran right into a barbed wire fence that cut his face. Or the time he cut his leg on the old wire fence. He tends to get injured often. I would say he is accident prone." Poli chuckled. "He seems to be afraid of nothing."

"That's what worries me, Poli. I think he's considering joining the war. Every time the radio is on, I watch him. And now, with the Japanese bombing Pearl Harbor, he is seething inside. I think our son is going to join the military."

"I've been wondering about that too. I don't think he'll sit around and wait to be drafted. He may be small, but he's tough and he's hardheaded. I don't know if we would be able to change his mind if he has decided to fight."

"Can't you talk to him about it, Poli? Man to man? And what about Raymond and George? What if they follow their older brother and decide to go too? I don't think I can handle having three sons go off to war. We've already lost two children plus the unborn." Alice took in a deep breath and let it out slowly. The memory of those losses still caused an ache in her heart after all those years.

"I will try, Alice, but I can't guarantee I will get through to him or if he'll even have a choice if a draft is called."

Days went by with people buzzing around town with the latest news. Neighbors discussed the events on the streets, at the market, at church, everywhere there was talk of war. Poli and Alice decided it was time to explain to their younger children what was happening because they asked many questions. Poli's and his sons' friends sometimes convened at his home to discuss the war, and the children were afraid. Alice asked Poli one night to go to one of the neighbor's homes who didn't have young children and discuss the war there instead.

The children didn't understand, yet they knew something was wrong. Their eyes widened as they watched their older brothers fiercely speak about fighting against the Japanese, the Germans, and the Italians. Oftentimes the little ones awakened in the night crying, and Alice comforted them until they fell asleep again. She prayed fervently for the nation, but especially for her sons, her family and neighbors, for peace in the world, and for evil to come to an end.

Each night as she knitted or patched up torn clothing by the woodstove, she prayed the rosary. If half of what she heard on the radio was true, the atrocities against human beings, especially Jewish people, was more barbaric than anything she had ever heard of before other than the Romans in the time of Jesus over nineteen hundred years ago and the white man against the Native American Indians. So night after night she prayed for the victims and their families. There were terrible rumors of brutal conflicts instigated by the Japanese on islands in the Pacific. Even at mass, the priest brought up the war and asked for prayers.

The men in Sanford and surrounding towns were joining the army, the navy, and the marines. Some young men were drafted, while others volunteered, hoping to put an end to the war quickly.

*   *   *

One evening in 1943, Alice's fears came to fruition as Pete announced he had signed up with the marines, and she felt as though she'd been punched in the stomach. Purposefully putting oneself in danger was not something she was accustomed to, and it was difficult to grasp.

Later Raymond enlisted in the navy, and George chose the army. Alice and Poli were relieved in a sense that their sons would be in separate areas of battle. Yet, if they had been together, they could have been supportive to each other and not alone hundreds or thousands of miles from home.

Mail was often delayed for months, and she had no word from her sons. Alice prayed nearly constantly for their safety and the safety of their other family members and neighbors. Never would she show tears or fear around her children, but at night when all were in bed, she wept quietly.

A few months later while the fighting continued around the world, Poli and Alice lay in their bed and discussed the horrors of war and which of their friends' sons didn't return home or returned home injured.

"One thing I am quite certain of, Roland won't be called to go with a missing thumb. That's if this war goes on for several more years." Poli scratched his head and rolled over to one side to face Alice.

"I guess that's one consolation," said Alice as she turned to face him. "I never thought I would actually be thankful he lost his thumb. I remember that day so well. It feels like it was yesterday, although it was a few months ago. It was such a difficult thing to go through for a fourteen-year-old boy. The saw sliced that thumb off before he had a chance to move his hand away. At first he was in shock, but as soon as he saw the blood, he screamed."

A tear escaped down her cheek as she vividly remembered the sight of that day and how Poli rushed him to the hospital, the thumb wrapped in a towel, hoping against hope the doctor could sew it back on somehow. Poli had arrived home hours later with a very pale teenage boy beside him. The doctor had stitched up the wound and wrapped it tightly, giving Poli instructions on how to clean it and change the bandages so they wouldn't risk infection.

Roland had cried himself to exhaustion and then sat at the table with barely enough energy to sit there without falling. Alice had quickly given him some milk and a little bit of food. She soothed him while he ate slowly. Once he had eaten, he asked if he could go to bed and lie down for a while. Alice had helped him up the stairs, removed his shoes, and tucked him under the blanket.

"Alice, you are quiet. What are you thinking?" Poli asked, and Alice returned to the present.

"I was just remembering that awful day when Roland lost his thumb. I felt so bad for him. I couldn't make it all better. He had a lot of pain for a few days even with the medicine. Do you remember how hard it was for him to button his shirts and tie his shoes in those days?"

"Oh yes, I remember. I wanted to do it for him, but I knew he had to learn to do it on his own even if it meant using his left hand instead, or getting frustrated and trying over and over again with the fingers on his right." He paused and thought for a moment. "I suppose it could be considered a blessing now if it keeps him from going to war."

"True. We never know what the future holds and why certain things happen, but God does. We just have to be faithful and trust He knows best. Even if that means our other sons go off to war to help others." Alice sighed and blinked away a few tears trying to escape.

"I suppose you're right, Alice. Let's leave it up to Him. Roland is strong and is a big help to me with the wood now that he's done with school. With the three oldest gone, I have been shorthanded, so I'm glad to have him here."

After Roland finished his schooling, he had begun working with his father in the logging business. He became quite efficient with using the saws and helping stack the wood along the side of the driveway. He was built much like his father—tall and lean. He enjoyed the outdoors and the smell of freshly cut wood. He especially loved to fish.

"Now let's get some sleep, Alice. I am exhausted."

"Good night, Poli," she said with a sigh.

"Good night, Alice."

Alice prayed a while longer secretly in her heart before drifting off to sleep.

Chapter Twenty-Six

CHRISTMAS: 1943

A couple of days before Christmas, a package arrived from the Red Cross. Alice couldn't imagine what they had sent in such a large box. The children were all anxious as bees on fresh blossoms to see what had been delivered to them. It was not often that packages arrived for them.

Ten-year-old Juliette stood quietly beside her mother while her siblings asked a million questions or tried to hurry their mother. Once the box was opened at the kitchen table, Alice began to read the labels on each present tucked inside. The eyes of the children were huge like their largest marbles. They were all talking at once.

"Is there a present for me?"

"Can I see in the box, Mama?"

"Who sent all this to us?"

Finally, Alice had to settle them down and said, "Okay children, quiet down now. I'm going as fast as I can. I'll hand you whatever present has your name on it. The Red Cross sent this package to us. They try to help out poor families at Christmas, and it looks like we were chosen this year."

"Henriette," she read the label.

Eleven-year-old Henriette quickly grabbed her gift. A nice, shiny black train could be seen through the plastic packaging. She quickly tore through it and exclaimed, "Look what I got! A train!"

"Can I see it?" asked Henri, who was a year older than his excited sister.

"You can look at it, but it's mine."

Alice called the other children's names and pulled out dolls, trucks, and baby toys.

"Henri, here's yours."

He spotted a bright, red truck about eight inches long, and his mouth practically dropped to the floor. He carefully took it from his mother's hands and admired his brand-new treasure. He temporarily forgot all about Henriette's train.

For the rest of the day and most of the next, the children played with their new toys. Henri cleaned and polished his truck daily and placed it on a shelf away from his siblings' hands. Henri could always tell when someone had played with it because they never cleaned it before placing it back on the shelf.

"Who played with my truck?" he asked one day, hands on hips. He looked around at the sea of faces, and not one admitted to it. In exasperation, he said, "I know one of you played with it 'cause it's dirty, so who was it?"

The culprit didn't dare come forward, and the innocent ones would not tattle, so they sat in silence.

"From now on you'd better ask me first if you want to play with it. I always take good care of your toys when I play with them." That said, he turned and walked out of the room. Alice had watched her children and hoped the guilty one would admit to his or her using the toy. They were whispering among themselves when she approached them.

"Children," she began and waited for their attention. "You know that Henri is right. Whenever he plays with any of your toys, he always cleans them and returns them as he found them. You don't always give him the same courtesy. From now on, you are not to touch his truck without his permission. Now, remember to treat each other's things as you would treat your own, with gentleness. I also expect you to tell the truth and admit to doing something so no one else takes the blame. Do you understand?"

They all nodded sheepishly.

"Good. Now tomorrow is Christmas and I need your help making pies. Adrienne, Henriette, Juliette, and Anita, please get the ingredients to make raisin pies and apricot pies and clear the table to make room. Roland, and Louie, I need you to get some wood and refill the wood box, plus I want you to shovel the snow from the doorways and steps. Papa is still plowing, so Roland and Louie, I also need you to make sure there's food for the dog and horse." As Henri reentered the room, she asked him to retrieve the eggs and feed the chickens.

"*Oui*, Mama," they said in unison. The older girls entered the pantry to get everything they needed and carried it back to the long kitchen table. Then they retrieved the bowls, utensils, and pie plates from the painted kitchen cabinets. The boys pulled on their coats, boots, hats, and mittens and headed outside.

Seven-year-old Shirley played with three-year-old Roger, keeping him away from their big sisters. Five-year-old Andre and six-year-old Ronald sat on the floor at the far end of the room, rolling marbles through gaps in a wooden board. Above each gap was a number penciled that showed the number of points they'd get if their marble passed through the opening. Of course these two were too young to read, so they simply cheered each time their marbles went through the holes.

Alice's short wavy hair was now highlighted with a few strands of grey, which she told her friends she'd earned raising so many children. She wore a light blue dress covered by a darker blue apron as she busily peeled and cut potatoes and onions and placed them in a large cauldron on the stove. As they sautéed in a small amount of water and butter, she pulled the hamburger out of the icebox, dropped it into her largest cast-iron frying pan, and placed it on one of the burners to cook. She put more wood into the woodstove using a doubled-up towel and lifted the lid, slowly dropping the wood into the fire. Later she would add the cooked hamburger to the cauldron and let the stew, called *chiarre*, simmer.

As she worked, Alice thought about her eldest son, Pete. He'd enlisted in the marines a few months ago and was off somewhere in the Pacific Ocean fighting the Japanese. Young men enlisted and were sent to various parts of the world to fight against the Japanese or the Nazi regime in Germany and surrounding countries. George was somewhere in Europe, and Raymond was probably at sea somewhere in the Pacific. It was their first Christmas away from home.

Alice prayed fervently for their safety every day as news of the war filtered in through the radio or newspapers. The mail was so sporadic because Pete fought in the jungles and he didn't receive mail for weeks, sometimes months, as it accumulated on base. She wrote to him often, telling him the news from home. When Pete would write, he would tell stories about meeting the natives and how they would teach the American soldiers how to survive.

The native women also taught the soldiers how to climb the coconut trees, since it was the women who were responsible for gathering those types of foods for their families. Pete said the bark on the trees had very sharp points on them and made pockets to allow rain in. However, if a person slipped while scaling the trees, he'd get cut up pretty badly. The climbers would have to squeeze the bark with their legs as they climbed.

Pete's buddy, Kelly, who was a happy-go-lucky, hillbilly type of guy, would scale the trees with Pete. Their marine buddies were afraid to climb because they didn't want to cut their legs. Pete and Kelly didn't care. They'd slip and get cut, but try again until they mastered it. They'd use a bayonet to cut the coconuts free from the tops of the trees and let them drop to the ground.

Pete said he liked the coconuts best when they were still green because they were tastier. Once they were back on the ground, they would retrieve the coconuts and the natives showed them how to cut off the thick exterior husk. He said it was impossible to do this if you didn't know what you were doing. The marines would use a bayonet to cut the tops off, drink the milk, and then cut out the interior meat. Pete also said that when the exterior of the coconut was spoiling, the milk inside would thicken like candy.

Alice could picture Pete getting his legs cut, but going on with more determination to conquer the tree. He had always gotten injured as a child and that's what worried her. He was not afraid to take risks, and she worried he'd get himself killed by the Japanese. So she prayed and let God take care of the rest.

Pete was careful not to disclose where they were in his letters; however, if he slipped and gave out too much information, his superiors would cut out those sections of the letters in the event they would fall into the hands of the enemy.

A loud scream brought Alice's mind back to the kitchen. She swung around to see Roger crying, big tears rolling down his face, and Shirley trying to comfort him.

"What happened?" Alice asked as she rushed to her toddler, picked him up, and held him gently, bouncing him up and down.

"He was climbing on the wood box and the wood rolled, and when he fell on the floor, some of the wood fell on top of him," a flustered Shirley said. "Sorry, Mama, I turned my back on him for just a minute."

Alice checked little Roger for injuries, saw none, kissed him on the cheek, and gently spoke to him. His sobs lessened to soft whimpers as he rested his head against his mother's shoulder.

"Don't worry, Shirley. Accidents happen and little children move fast." Alice sat in the rocker beside the woodstove gently rocking her tiny son. In a few minutes, Roger was squirming to get down and play, so she lowered him to the floor, and he ran toward Andre and Ronald who were still playing marbles.

Shirley picked up the wood and restacked the box, which her older brothers had recently filled. The older girls resumed their work with their pie making, and Alice walked to the sink to wash her hands and then placed the food in the cauldron.

"Mama, how do you like our pie crusts?" asked Adrienne. Alice came over to the table and looked over Juliette's shoulder to inspect their creations.

"You girls are doing a great job. Keep up the good work and don't forget to pinch the edges of the crusts."

"We won't. After that do you want us to put the fillings in?"

"Do you have them all ready, Anita?" Alice had gone over to where the boys were playing, since an argument had begun. The bigger boys weren't too happy with Roger, who grabbed their marbles as they rolled them toward the board. Alice picked up her son, removed the marbles from his tight grip, and handed them to Ronald. With Roger in her arms, she turned her attention back to the girls.

"*Oui*, Mama. The fillings are in the bowls on the counter."

"*Bien*, then go ahead and fill them like I showed you. When you're done, we'll put them in the oven." Still holding on to Roger, she walked down the narrow hall to the back door to check on the older boys. She passed coat hooks and boots lined against the right wall. She heard the girls giggling about something that happened at school yesterday. Alice opened the solid wood door and peered outside. It was still snowing lightly; however, the boys had shoveled the path near the door and around the bulkhead door leading to the cellar.

"Hmmm, they must be out front now," she said to the toddler, who played with the buttons on her dress. She closed the door and walked past the girls in the kitchen, opened the living room door, and closed it behind her. She opened the front door on the far right and walked out onto the enclosed front porch and saw the boys just finishing up the front steps. Even though they rarely used the front steps, they kept them shoveled off in case they'd need to use them as an emergency exit if there was ever a fire.

She felt the laundry hanging on the porch and the pieces were stiff. Later on she'd take them in and allow them to finish drying on the clothes racks in the cellar. As she stepped back into the living room and closed the porch door, she took a few minutes to look around the small, comfortable room. To her left was a small sofa against the staircase wall and to her right near the front windows were two stuffed chairs. Against the opposite wall was a piano, which she played a few times a year when company came for a visit and would sing a few songs. A rocking chair and a wooden chair along with a lamp table flanked the center wall separating the kitchen.

Black-and-white photos were displayed over wallpapered walls, and an area rug covered the center of the clean linoleum floor. The room stayed clean since the children were not allowed to play in there. So many memories washed through her mind like rain running down a gutter. She took a long, deep breath and returned to the kitchen, young Roger balanced on her hip.

"Are the pies ready, girls?"

"Look, Mama, what do you think?" asked Juliette.

"Hmmm, let me look." The girls waited anxiously for their mother's approval as they snuck peeks at each other.

"They look perfect. You all did a great job. Now let's get them in the oven." She placed Roger on the floor and gave him a pan and spoon to play with. She carefully placed two pies on each oven rack, slid the racks in, and closed the oven door.

"They'll be ready in about half an hour. Don't forget them."

"We won't."

Alice took the most recent letter from Pete out of her apron pocket and sat in her rocker to read it.

"Mama, is that a letter from Pete?" asked Juliette as she knelt by her mother's chair.

"Yes, it is."

"Is he hurt? Did he say anything about the Japanese?"

"He said he's fine and that the Japs are tough and cruel, and he hopes he never gets captured by them. He's seen a lot of killing but he doesn't talk too much about it. War is a terrible thing."

"Will Pete die, Mama?"

"I hope not, Juliette. I pray for him all the time that the good Lord will protect him."

"Me, too. Did he talk about the natives again?"

"Oh yes, he tells stories about what they teach the soldiers to survive in the jungles, and what is safe to eat and not safe. They are happy to help because they want them to defeat the Japanese."

"Where is he now?"

"He can't say, except he's on an island in the Pacific Ocean, which is very far from here. He said it's hot out there even in December."

"Did you get a letter from George?"

"Not for a while. He's still fighting in France as far as I know. Maybe we will get a letter from him soon. I pray for him every day, too."

"What about Raymond? Any letter from him?"

"No, not this time. Who knows, he may be in the Pacific near Pete. They wouldn't know that since there's no way for them to reach each other. The only news they get is from us at home. Sometimes long gaps of time go by before he gets a letter, and by then he has many piled up."

They talked for a bit while keeping a watch on the oven and the other children. Alice got up and opened the oven door slightly to check on the pies, letting out tantalizing scents of raisin pie and apricot pie.

"Mmmmm, are the pies done?" asked Henri, as he came in with a few dozen eggs. He licked his lips in anticipation. *That boy is always hungry,* thought Alice, chuckling quietly.

"Just about."

"Can I have a piece, Mama?"

"Well, Henri, they'll need to cool a bit first. Why don't we wait so you won't spoil your supper, and besides we need to save some for tomorrow, which is Christmas, remember?"

"Oh Mama! I'll be able to eat just the same."

That's my hungry boy for sure, she thought. Five minutes later she put Pete's letter back into her apron pocket, removed the pies from the oven, and placed them on pot holders to cool.

The older boys came inside after they finished shoveling and removed their winter gear by the back door. Their faces were as red as fire trucks, and the static made their hair stand on end after they removed their wool hats. Their sisters teased them about looking like porcupines.

Christmas day arrived with a spectacular sunrise bursting with bright orange and yellow streaks across the eastern sky. The Alexandre family was always up early, starting their chores even before the sun rose on winter days. Alice would awaken early and begin the day's preparations. Although the family was self-sufficient in providing wood for the stove, canned foods from their garden to last through the winter, eggs from the fifty or so chickens in the coop, cows for milk and meat, there was little extra money to provide for gifts for such a large brood.

Alice had purchased oranges and placed an orange at each place setting for her children. This was a treat for them since they didn't eat oranges the rest of the year. Some years she would give them each an apple as well. She made a large bowl of crepe mixture for a special breakfast and started cooking them on the stove. She piled them on a plate nearby to keep warm while she fed the little children before the older ones came in from the barn.

Napoleon and Roland milked the cows. Henri's stomach somersaulted at the thought of doing that task as did Juliette's. Both felt it was gross collecting milk from a cow's udders. Henriette liked the outdoor work better than the household chores so she assisted in milking the cows. Raymond had married Florence the year before, and they lived next door in a tiny house and sometimes joined them for meals. Henri helped feed the cows, horses, and pigs, then collected the eggs and went in for breakfast. The girls helped their mother with setting the table, feeding the younger children, and serving the males before sitting down to their own breakfast.

Once the dishes were cleaned, the family went to Holy Family Church for the Christmas mass. The rest of the day they played with their new, but limited toys or went outside to play in the snow.

Alice was six months pregnant for her seventeenth child, but she was a strong woman and worked from early morning until late in the evening. By this time she had two miscarriages and lost two young children, Adrian and Edgar. Even on Christmas day she had no time for rest since her family still needed to be fed three meals a day. She worked without complaining and accepted the fact that this was what was needed to care for her family. Napoleon took a nap in the afternoon as he did on

Sundays, but Alice never took a nap. She always said the Lord gave her the strength she needed every day.

Odile and Pierre visited as well as Alexandrine, Alma, John, and their families. Alexandrine had married her stepfather's brother, Arthur Laprise, and they had two children, John and Arthur, Jr. Alma married Lucien Laitres when she was in her late thirties. Their children were Pauline and Richard. John was still unmarried; however, he was courting Blandine Hebert. Alice's sister Henedine, who had been engaged to be married, had died at the age of twenty-nine. Her half-brothers, Henry and Edgar, were also married and often stopped by for short visits. Yvonne was not married, and Annette married Roger Morin later in life and had no children.

During times like Christmas, other holidays, and family gatherings, they reminisced about their younger years. Alice's aunts and uncles would join them on occasion; however, they usually met at Odile and Pierre's home. Albert married Louise Lizotte, and Elisa married Horace Richard and had eight children. Arthur's first wife died young after they had two children, and he married a widow and they had a daughter. Fabien also married a Lizotte girl, and they had three children; however, they tragically lost their young daughter when she was run over by a truck. Alice married a Lizotte, and they had three children. The three Lizottes were siblings. Alfred married and moved to Massachusetts and had five children.

Poli did not see his family very often as they remained in Canada. He visited only a couple of times. His family was too large for him to afford to travel that far. Some of his siblings also had large families which made it difficult for them to travel into Maine due to costs. They communicated by letters until they could afford a telephone. His two bachelor brothers, Eugene and Louie, traveled to Maine a few times, and Poli's family caught up on the news of the rest of the family and shared many laughs.

During these visits they invited friends to gather in the living room and Alice would play the piano. Her favorite song was "Good Old Summer Time." She often hummed or sang while cooking or washing dishes.

* * *

Winter flew by and spring arrived bringing strong winds and still more snow. As usual, in Maine the temperatures fluctuated, teasing people that spring-like weather was getting close. Alice prayed there wouldn't be a snowstorm when baby number seventeen decided it was time to meet his or her family. The girls and Alice had begun spring cleaning earlier in the month by cleaning out cobwebs and dust from the walls and under the beds upstairs. On the warmer days, they emptied dresser drawers and the small closets to wash the insides. They reorganized the clothes, moving the spring and summer clothes closer to the front. Each child didn't have much clothing, but there were so many of them that moving clothes that no longer fit the older children into the younger children's dressers was a chore.

Once the upstairs was complete, they moved to the lower floor. The work was easier with many hands helping. As March progressed, Alice felt the weight of her unborn child drop, and she recognized the time was near for her to give birth once again. Alice was a few months shy of forty-four years old with a few strands of grey in her shiny black hair. Her daughter, Adrienne, would turn seventeen in April and was a great help around the house. Henriette would be eleven on the thirty-first of the month. Juliette was almost ten, and Anita a year behind her. Shirley was only seven years old but a help just the same. Alice felt terrible that she needed to depend so much on Adrienne; however, she didn't have a choice. There was so much to do, and the boys mainly helped with the outdoor chores. The family arose early each day to tackle all the chores that needed to be done.

On March 26, 1943, Gerard came into the world. He was born at Henrietta D. Goodall Hospital rather than at home. The girls assisted their mother with caring for the newborn, the cooking, baking, and cleaning. The boys joined their dad with barn chores, clearing snow, sawing wood, and loading it into the basement or into the back of his truck to deliver to their customers. Alice sent a letter to her sons informing them they had a new brother. Letters from her sons at war were few and far between; however, she wrote to them as often as she could.

The fighting continued spreading throughout Europe, Asia, and the Pacific islands. In one letter from Pete, he informed them he had been cut across his mouth by a Japanese soldier. He said he was fine and had been stitched up and returned to the jungle to fight. George was somewhere in Germany or France, and Raymond was home after being discharged. The V-mail (victory mail) they received was sporadic and never truly identified where they were as precautions from the enemies.

Chapter Twenty-Seven

1944: ONE LAST PREGNANCY

The year passed quickly and Napoleon drove Alice to Goodall Hospital in January of 1944 for another baby delivery. This time she didn't make it to full term, and her twin daughters, Therese and Marie Rolande, were born prematurely. Therese weighed three pounds and Rolande weighed one and a half pounds. The doctor and nursing staff were unable to save the life of Marie Rolande. Another devastating loss was suffered by Alice, Poli, and their family. Alice wept softly as she held the lifeless body of her youngest child. A nurse called the Alexandre home and asked Poli to return to the hospital. The staff worked day and night to keep Therese alive, and she survived. Alice returned home with her tiny bundle, and with the help of her daughters, they fed and cared for this precious little baby who was so tiny.

Once she was strong enough, Alice sent another letter to her sons informing them they had two little sisters and that one had not made it. She also told them the doctor told her and Poli it was too dangerous for her to continue having children. Her body was worn out and should she get pregnant again, either she or the baby, or both, would not survive. Alice had given birth to a total of nineteen children and miscarried two. It was finally time to stop, build her strength, and care for the sixteen remaining. Fortunately some were adults and able to care for themselves. Raymond and Florence had a child of their own, and if he survived the war, perhaps more children would come. Alice figured that being a grandmother and a mother at the same time was time-consuming enough, and she was relieved that she would no longer have to bear children.

The days ran into weeks and months as Therese's little body strengthened and grew, and with each passing day, Alice and Poli relaxed a bit more, praying and feeling she would survive. Her elder siblings cared for and nurtured her while watching her progress. The baby must have felt their love because she continued to blossom under their watchful care. By the time March arrived, she had gained several pounds. Her tiny legs and arms wiggled around like leaves blowing in the wind, and she smiled happily each time her siblings approached her crib.

Alice loved the way each newborn child was accepted by his or her siblings and never did she sense jealousy when a new one arrived. She had heard that sometimes older siblings were jealous of the time and attention the youngest one inevitably received; however, her family adjusted well. It was what they always knew.

*   *   *

One day when the mail arrived, Alice retrieved the letters from the box by the roadside and recognized Pete's V-mail. She tore it open as she walked up the driveway to the back door. Chuckling, she read Pete's comments about all the babies being born while he has been away and asked, "What the heck is going on over there?" He continued by telling her that a year's worth of mail had finally reached him, so he sorted the letters by date before reading them. In one letter she told him about Gerard being born, and in another letter she'd told him about the twin girls born ten months later. Alice laughed out loud as she could picture his reaction as he read letter after letter.

Pete had suffered his second injury, and this time it was more severe. He had been shot in the leg by machine gun in Guam and sent to a hospital in New Caledonia for surgery. There were about seventy men in each ward. They spoke French in that area, so he felt at home. At one time during his stay, he asked a nurse for a bottle of liquor and she said she couldn't do that.

He said, "Sure you can. Just go out to the fence and ask the natives." The fence was built around the hospital to keep the natives out. The nurse refused so he went over and bought a bottle. The nurses were furious with him so they asked the doctor about it. The doctor said it was fine because he was a former combat soldier and he took a shot glass and passed it around. Pete said he liked that doctor.

After that period in the hospital, Pete was sent to California for six months for rehabilitation, then to Connecticut and to North Carolina. He wrote that he didn't enjoy it at all. He said he wanted to go back and fight the Japs, but the major said he couldn't. Pete signed up for the Cooks and Bakers School since he couldn't get into the mechanics program. When he was asked to cook for the officers, he said, "No, I don't cook for special diets." Alice said to herself, *that's my son!*

A few weeks later, a letter from George arrived. His letters never made her laugh. Although he did not speak much about the war, she read between the lines and could tell he had seen some horrific deaths in Germany and France. She felt the army was not the place for this son. She prayed even more fervently for his well-being—emotionally, physically, and spiritually. He was on the ground fighting in areas where some of the fiercest reinforcements were fighting according to the news broadcasts. She prayed he would survive these battles.

From Raymond she heard of silly things the men did aboard ship to keep from thinking about the war twenty-four hours a day; however, they were always on their guard for torpedoes and enemy ships and planes. Their ship moved around a lot to keep from being detected by their enemies. She still had no idea if he was in the Pacific or Atlantic

Ocean because, like her two other sons, the mail could get intercepted and their location would be in jeopardy.

By early 1945, all three sons had returned home from war. Although they were alive, Alice sensed, at least with George, that a part of them died while they were away. Pete spent a great deal of time talking about his adventures and injuries, and she felt this was his way of coping and healing. George never discussed it, and therefore the healing wasn't taking place in his mind and heart. Raymond talked about some of what went on, but he was not as vocal as his eldest brother. Alice felt they just wanted to put it all behind them and not have to relive it. She didn't pursue it. If they wished to talk, then she would listen, but until then, she would just love and pray for them.

The news reported that in 1945, on the thirtieth of April, Adolf Hitler committed suicide as Soviet forces encircled the German capital of Berlin. The American troops had crossed the Rhine River on March 7. On May 7, the Germans surrendered to the western Allies at Reims, and on May 9, they surrendered to the Soviets in Berlin. In August, the war in the Pacific ended soon after the United States dropped atomic bombs on the Japanese cities of Hiroshima and Nagasaki killing 120,000 civilians. The Japanese surrendered on September 2. In total there was an estimated 55 million deaths worldwide resulting from World War II.

Alice and Poli, along with their family, friends, and neighbors, thanked the Lord God the war was finally over. They were especially thankful their three sons returned home alive and prayed this would be the end of wars.

Chapter Twenty-Eight

FIRE OF 1947

The spring of 1947 was an extremely wet one for the people of the grand state of Maine; however, by the end of June the rains stopped. The summer was hot and dry for most of the state and continued that way into the autumn. By the time October arrived, the ground was so dry that wells, streams, and brooks had dried up, leaving the area in a very dangerous situation. The possibility of fire erupting was foremost in the mind of fire personnel, game wardens, hunters, and many other people. Unfortunately there were others who paid no attention to the signs and warnings and continued to hunt, smoke cigarettes, and log lumber.

Joseph "Pete" Alexandre had returned home from the war nearly three years prior and worked with his dad selling wood in places as far away as Alton Bay, New Hampshire, for furniture and other uses. Hunting season had begun in parts of the state and was due to begin on November 1 in the southern counties. The hunters, the loggers, and all others who spent time in the woods looked around them and noticed how incredibly dry the brush, pine needles, dead branches, grass, and the ground had become. Governor Hildreth and State Fire Inspector Lawrence Dolby considered not allowing hunting season until they would get rain. The fire danger was at a class 4 stage in southern Maine.

Pete entered the house one day in October and reported fires had started in New Hampshire near Ossipee and were headed into Newfield, Maine. Volunteers were needed to help evacuate people and their belongings. Others were needed to combat the fires. Training was available for those willing to risk their lives fighting the fires. Command posts were being set up in various parts of the county.

After much discussion, Poli, Pete, George, and Roland prepared the truck for transporting people and their furnishings. Alice hung rosaries around the house to protect their home should the winds turn the fire in their direction.

The men headed to Waterboro, and Pete stayed with the fire crews to help fight the fires that had reached the area. The others were directed to the roads that needed evacuation first. When Pete returned home at the end of one day he said, "We fought the fire from the road that went from Waterboro to Ross Corner (West Road) in the area of the Massabesic Forest. The fire was traveling too fast at one time, we couldn't get to it. It would burn the roots and start up again elsewhere. The extremely strong winds drove the fire. We'd be fighting the fire in one place, and a mile or so away, someone would see another one start up. We had to divert the fire so that it would not go to Alfred Road. We saved an old farm on top of a hill where there was an orchard."

Alice looked at her son, covered head to toe with black ash, and said, "Let's discuss this after you wash up just like your father and brothers." Pete scrubbed layers of soot and ash from his hair down to his feet. Although he'd worn his handkerchief around his nose and mouth, he still coughed up soot. He rolled his clothes up and walked outside to shake them out before putting them in with his dad's and brothers' laundry. When he returned, he continued his story, and his father and brothers added their stories as well.

"We had these Indian-style fire extinguishers on our backs, but they didn't help much," Pete said. "As soon as we had one fire out, another started a hundred feet away. We weren't sure if someone was out there starting fires, but then we realized in our area that the fire was burning underground, following the roots and starting up in another spot."

Poli joined in, "As we were loading up people's belongings into the truck, we watched as fire jumped from the treetops onto other trees and spread fast. The fire was bouncing all over the place." Poli took a bite of a sandwich and drank some milk. "We need to go back out there. There are so many homes being lost. The fire was headed toward Lyman and Kennebunk, and they need help. If the wind would only stop, the firefighters might have a chance to get this under control. It's a monster."

Alice asked, "What can we do here? What happens if the fire turns in this direction? I see smoke toward Lebanon too. I won't have any way to get the children out of here with you gone."

"Pray, Alice, that's all we can do, is pray. Have Henriette, Juliette, Anita, and Louie throw buckets of water on the sides of the house if it looks like the fire is headed your way. We also heard of people putting wet blankets on their roofs. Maybe some of the neighbor boys could help with that."

George piped in and said, "We can have the L'Heureuxs or the Genests come and get you if it looks like the fire will shift this way. Right now it's in Shapleigh, Waterboro, Lyman, and headed toward the Kennebunk area. There's no way of knowing what it will do next."

Poli, George, Raymond, Roland, and Henri finished eating and traveled in Poli's truck to continue to move people and some of their belongings from their homes before the fires reached them. They helped many families in Waterboro evacuate the area. The difficulty was finding a place for them to go and not knowing where the fire was headed next. Pete drove back to Waterboro to fight the fires.

The fire continued for a week, burning homes and businesses in its wake. Fires were reported to have hit Bar Harbor and Acadia National Park, Machias, as far north as Anson and Carmel, and down to York County.

A few days after the fire was extinguished, Pete drove out to survey the damage and noted that many of the large chicken farms in Newfield and Limerick that he used to deliver shavings to when he worked for Gendron Lumber had all burned in the fire. The losses were incredible. The miracles were also amazing as the fire would be headed straight for a farmhouse and at the last minute, veer off and that farm was saved. Roland, who enjoyed fishing, headed to Kennebunk Pond in Lyman to survey the damage, and he reported only four structures were left unharmed.

Juliette, now a fourteen-year-old girl, explained to her brothers and father how they could smell the smoke all around them. "We were so afraid that it would come to Sanford. All we could see and smell was smoke." They learned that fires burned in Lebanon, Alfred, Lyman, Shapleigh, Wells, Newfield, Waterboro, Arundel, Kennebunk, Kennebunkport, Biddeford, and many other southern Maine towns. Sanford residents thought it would eventually come to them. Juliette said, "Thank God Mom hung rosaries all around the house so our house would not burn. We prayed a lot and we were scared. The smoke was everywhere."

That winter following the devastating fires, Roland decided to go ice fishing at Kennebunk Pond. When he returned home he reported, "The wind blew so cold because there were no trees to block it. It was freezing out there. Just the four houses and a few trees are left. It looks so bare." A few men who owned property at Kennebunk Pond had watered down their homes and then got into a boat and went out to the middle of the pond to escape the flames. The smoke was so heavy that they almost died from inhalation and realized they had done a very stupid thing. Their lives were saved as well as their property, but it was a risk they should not have taken.

Unfortunately there were some fatalities, although not as many as they had feared. Some of the people who rushed to the ocean for safety died from burning lungs. They were trapped by the ocean behind them and the fire in front of them.

Chapter Twenty-Nine

PETU, THE NEIGHBOR: 1948

Ronald, Andre, and Louie had hoisted their homemade bats onto their shoulders as they strutted out of the barn and were heading toward the driveway. They spotted their neighbor, Ron, nicknamed Petu, heading in their direction.

"*Bonjour*, Petu," yelled Ronald, "you want to play baseball?" Petu was a nervous boy, an only child, yet he enjoyed playing with his neighbors. He ran across the lawn, anxious to join his friends in a fun game of baseball.

"*Bonjour*," he responded upon reaching the small group. "Where are your other brothers?"

"The older ones are helping Papa in the woods today. He bought another wood lot so he needed them to cut down trees. The younger ones are with Mama in the house. We can still play with four of us," said Louie.

"All right. Where do you want me to be? First base?"

"Yeah, you can play first base," said Ronald. "Louie can be up at bat first. I'll go between second and third base, and Andre can pitch."

Ronald threw the ball underhanded to Andre; it bounced once and Andre caught it. The bats were thrown on the ground behind home base, and Louie chose his favorite. The "bases" consisted of whatever they could find available, usually a piece of wood or a large rock. Once all the players were in position, Andre pitched the first ball of the first inning. The ball soared over little Louie's head and he ran to catch it. He threw it back to his brother and waited for the next pitch.

The second pitch lined up between his knees and chest so he swung with all his might and it connected with the bat. The ball flew straight to first base; however, Petu missed it and it rolled behind him toward the wood pile. Louie ran as fast as his young legs would go and tapped his foot on first base. Andre said, "Keep going, Louie. Go to second base." Petu reached the ball and threw it to Andre at the pitcher's mound.

"Good hit, Louie," said Ronald. "Who wants to bat next?"

"I will," said Petu. He jogged over to home base, grabbed a bat, and stood in position. Meanwhile Ronald moved his position closer to first base.

Andre wound his arm and threw the pitch right into the dirt and it bounced into the tree line behind Petu. Petu ran to retrieve it and threw it back to Andre. Louie was inching his way to third base when Andre threw the next pitch. Petu swung and missed. Louie ran to third base while Petu ran for the ball. When Andre looked over his shoulder in his direction, Louie shrugged and smiled big. Andre shook his head and laughed.

"Okay, Petu, are you ready?" shouted Andre.

"Yes I am. Go ahead." The pitch was wide but Petu swung again for his second strike. He dragged the bat along as he strolled over to the ball.

"Try again, Petu," said Louie. "Bring me home."

On the third try, Petu hit a ground ball that rolled past Andre toward second base and Ronald ran quickly to retrieve it as Petu sprinted to first base and Louie touched home base. The boys were laughing now and having a terrific time, but with only four boys playing, it was impossible to cover all the bases and an outfield. The thrill of the game was what they enjoyed, so they played like that for the next hour until their thirst increased. The brothers invited their friend into the house to get some milk. Mama turned toward them as they entered the kitchen and she smiled.

"*Bonjour*, Petu. How are you today?" Alice asked.

"I'm good, Madame Alexandre. How are you today?" He looked around the kitchen and surveyed the younger children playing.

Before Alice could answer, she heard Ronald say, "Mama, we're thirsty. Could we have some milk please?"

"Yes, of course. Would you all like a cookie?" Alice laughed as they quickly answered in the affirmative. She had never seen young children turn down a cookie. Once the Alexandre boys had finished, they dashed back outside, while Petu asked to use the bathroom.

Ronald, being rather mischievous at times, got an idea so he whispered to his brothers, "Boys, you know how Petu's mother is always making him do girl stuff right?" The boys nodded. "Well, I think we need to toughen him up a bit so he doesn't become a sissy." He told them his plan, and they put it into action when Petu joined them.

"Let's go play in the woods now, Petu. I'm tired of playing ball," said Ronald. Off they trudged into the wooded area behind their house, chatting about the ball game and other fun times they had together. They wandered further into the tree line so Mama wouldn't spot them. A rotted oak tree had fallen to the ground during a thunderstorm and lay across their path. Ronald decided this was the place to put his plan into action.

"Petu, we're going to play hide-and-seek now. You sit here on this old tree and wait until we yell that we're ready, okay?"

"Okay, Ronnie," he said trustingly.

Ronald, Andre, and Louie ran swiftly out of the woods back into their yard. Ronald whispered to them and said, "Let's see how long he stays there." They waited and waited and didn't hear or see Petu. The boys played ball and laughed for the next hour and still no sign of Petu.

Andre was concerned that he may be hurt, but Ronald said he was fine and not to worry. A while later, the boys heard Petu's mother calling for him. They lived in the house next door and heard her loud and clear calling for her son. The boys snuck around the tall wood pile and ran into the woods without being spotted by Madame Perreault. Tripping over downed branches and tree roots, they hurried toward where they had left Petu and found him still seated on the log.

"Where have you guys been? What took you so long?" he asked, clearly stunned.

"Sorry Petu. Your mother is calling for you," said Andre.

Petu asked again, "Where were you? Did you leave me there on purpose?" He stared at his friends and waited. Andre and Louie looked at Ronald and gave him a look that said *you'd better answer that question since this was your idea.*

Ronald cleared his throat and said, "Well, it's like this. We wanted to see how you would act by yourself. We wanted to toughen you up." The other boys defended themselves and revealed it was Ronald's idea, and they were sorry they went along with it.

Petu followed the boys out of the woods in silence, relieved to be headed home.

Days later, Petu joined his neighbors, pretending he'd forgotten about their mean trick. He never told his mother, so the boys didn't get into trouble. Andre and Louie apologized once Ronald was out of earshot. Petu shrugged and said, "That's okay. I know you didn't want to be mean to me. Let's play, okay?"

The younger boys' faces showed relief as they padded across the yard to where Henri and Ronald stacked four-foot logs along the driveway's edge. Their father and elder brothers had arrived with a truckload of wood hauled out of his most recently purchased wood lot. Petu asked why the wood was piled further away from the other rows of wood.

Poli responded, "Well, Petu, this wood is still green, which means it's still wet. It needs time to dry out to be any good for burning. We keep it in a separate area so that it doesn't get mixed up with the dry wood."

The youngster pondered this information for a moment and very seriously asked, "Then what happens when it rains on the other wood? Do you have to move it over?"

Poli chuckled, which confused the boy, and explained that the wood has moisture in it and the air dries it out on the inside. "Sometimes we cover up the dry pile so the outside doesn't get wet, because it is harder to get a fire going. Do you understand?" Poli looked down at the boy and puffed on his pipe, swirls of smoke drifting upwards over his head.

Finally Petu said, "I think so, Monsieur Alexandre. The old pile is still dry on the inside but the green pile isn't. Right?"

"Right, Petu. You're catching on." He patted the boy's head and winked, and Petu smiled big. Poli, Henri, and Ronald continued piling the wood while the younger ones ran off to play. Ronald released a sigh, and Poli asked, "What was that about?"

Ronald didn't mean to sigh loudly and quickly said, "Oh nothing, Papa, just taking a breath." Poli studied his son a few moments and wondered why he'd looked relieved about something as soon as Petu ran off to play. He was aware his son tended to be mischievous. Perhaps he had done something to Petu and was nervous Petu would tattle on him. He shrugged, scratched his head, and set his hat back on, figuring he may never find out and perhaps that was for the best. Petu didn't act agitated or angry, so most likely he'd already forgiven Ronnie for whatever he had guilty feelings about.

Chapter Thirty

SPRING 1949

On one unusually quiet April afternoon in the Alexandre home, Alice rocked back and forth in her favorite chair by the wood-burning stove. A pair of torn trousers sat on her lap as she threaded her needle. Five-year-old Therese napped in the adjoining room, the other young children had not yet arrived from school, and the eldest were either at their jobs or with their spouses in their own homes. Poli would be home around 5:00 p.m.

Alice turned toward the west-facing window, catching a glimpse of the remaining snow. April tended to be a month of varying weather patterns and temperature fluctuations. Already by the fourth week, Sanford had its share of contrasts. Two ferocious blizzards dumped sixteen inches of snow. In between them, temperatures rose to sixty degrees with longer daylight hours improving the morale of everyone. Hope was in the air as friends, family, and neighbors smiled to each other while out walking or in their yards as spring pushed the winter blues away.

Everyone knew the snow wouldn't last long at this time of year. It was an inconvenience for vehicles and pedestrians; however, the sight of tiny purple crocuses popping through the softening ground lightened the mood, and Alice understood new life was upon them again.

In two months she would hit the fifty-year mark of her birth day. Touches of grey streaked her dark wavy hair and a few wrinkles formed near her eyes. As her fingers wove the needle through the patch in the torn knees of Gerard's trousers, she thought of her grandparents and great-grandparents, now gone, and how each life affects so many others in simple, small, or sometimes large and extraordinary ways.

Fifty years ago, her mother was a frightened sixteen-year-old girl carrying her first child and never anticipating she'd become a widow at age twenty-one with four children to feed. Nor did she ever anticipate leaving her Canadian homeland and traveling to Sanford, Maine, reuniting with her grandparents, parents, and siblings. Later she remarried, to Pierre Laprise, who was a traveling salesman for S. B. Emery, and she gave birth to five more children. Odile had become a very strong person by necessity. She died in her early sixties from a contagious disease. Alice missed her mother terribly and often thought of her. Her stepfather visited the family as often as he could.

Alice bent to retrieve another article of clothing from her mending basket, threaded her needle, and commenced the repetitive sewing in and out of the cloth before tying a knot in the last stitch. She thought of Poli and their nearly twenty-nine years of marriage. How handsome and tall he was when she first glimpsed him at her great-grandparents' home where they boarded other Canadians coming to work in the mills. *Funny,* she thought, *Poli and I take in boarders too, even though we have a houseful of children.*

Mr. Genest and Mr. Roy had been boarders who arrived from Canada seeking employment. Mr. Genest eventually purchased land across the street. *God has His plans and they are amazing. Helping out people so they can have a fresh start and buy land for a home or a business is a neighborly thing to do and what God calls us to do. Just goes to show you that a little kindness goes a long way.*

Her thoughts settled on their firstborn, Joseph "little Pete," now nearly twenty-eight years of age, who announced he would be getting married in September to Evelyn Woodman. He was a little spitfire, and she smiled as she thought Evelyn would have her hands full. Her second child, Raymond, now married more than seven years, had children of his own. George, her third son, had married Dorothy Johnson almost two years before and they had one son.

Her eldest daughter, Adrienne, worked long hours in the mills and helped out at home. Alice prayed that Adri would find a husband who would care for her and be helpful around the home because she deserved it after all the work she's had to do being the eldest girl. The pain of losing her twin, Adrien, and the next one in line, Edgar, still brought sadness to Alice's heart even after all these years.

As Alice continued weaving her needle through the next article of clothing, a pair of Poli's socks, her thoughts continued with her next child, Roland, now nineteen years old, tall and handsome, and a hard worker. She remembered the day he lost his thumb and how she wished there was something else she could have done for him. Fortunately that accident led to him not going to war. She sighed and reminisced about how particular her Henri was and liked everything orderly. *Was it just the other day when Roland picked up manure and threw it against the barn walls that Henri had just finished cleaning?*

Then there was Henriette at age fifteen, still preferring fishing and outdoor chores to housework. Alice wondered if she would be able to marry her off anytime in the near future. Juliette, the tenth child, and Anita, the eleventh, had become very capable helpers with the household chores and with the younger children. Alice wondered how she would get along without them once they were off and married. Hopefully that would be a few more years yet. Louie, with his round face and nice smile, was a little charmer, and Alice enjoyed listening to his stories.

Choosing another pair of socks, this pair belonging to Roger, she again threaded her needle and began the repetitive motion she could do in her sleep. Alice wondered how much money she would have earned had she been paid for every piece of clothing she had darned over the years. She stood up and stretched and placed another chunk of wood into the stove before sitting back down and continuing her reverie as she stitched.

Where was I? Oh yes, Shirley. I think she may become a nun someday the way she talks about the Sisters and praying to Jesus. That's good. I'd like to have at least one child enter a religious vocation, she said to herself. Alice smiled again at the thought of her mischievous son, Ronald, and how he was always up to something. Like the time he picked on poor Petu and the other neighborhood boys. *What am I going to do with him?*

Ten-year-old Andre was next in her thoughts. Alice pictured his long, curly hair and slim build and how he loved to play ball or go sledding in the winter and did not enjoy having her cut his hair. Roger, with his round face and twinkly eyes, always made his mother smile with his good-natured personality. He could also scare her with creepy things he'd collect in his pockets. And then Gerard, who was probably watching the antics of his older brother, Ronald, and trying a few out for size was full of surprises.

Lastly, Alice thought of her youngest, Therese, now age five, with straight dark hair, who was beginning to be a little helper at home, and her twin sister, Marie Rolande, who died at birth. Rocking back and forth, Alice saw how in some ways the time passed so quickly yet she had often wondered while she toiled how she would get through a particularly difficult day or through the incredible loss of a child, not just once but three times (or more accurately five times if one counted the two miscarriages as well).

Alice knew one thing for certain. If she hadn't had faith in her God and His Son, Jesus, she never would have made it through all the trials without the strength from above. Life, though not easy, is worth living especially knowing there is a purpose for each person on this earth. If we have a relationship with our Creator, we know we will someday see Him face-to-face. The glory of heaven awaits all those who put their trust in Him, for He loves us so.

Alice found comfort in knowing this important truth and closed her eyes and prayed again for each one of her children and the future that lay ahead for them.

ABOUT THE AUTHOR

Irene Cote Single, a Maine native, has sold real estate for over 3 decades, works part-time to pursue writing. She had written a local column for 2 years in a weekly paper and volunteers on church committees. As a new author she is trusting in God to help her continue her dream of writing. She lives in Maine with her husband and daughter.

CPSIA information can be obtained at www.ICGtesting.com
Printed in the USA
BVOW07s0853270814

364383BV00002B/5/P